MISTLETOE AND MIREWORTH

A MANNERS AND MONSTERS CHRISTMAS NOVELLA

TILLY WALLACE

ISBN 978-0-473-60433-2

Published by Ribbonwood Press

To be the first to hear about new releases, sign up at:

https://www.tillywallace.com/newsletter

1

Autumn ushered in the busiest months Hannah could ever remember, even though the social season had officially ended. Over a period of weeks, Hannah and Wycliff journeyed repeatedly to the Duat and searched for the trapped *ka* of the Afflicted. Word spread among the *ton* and at odd times (normally dusk or dawn) a quiet knock on the door would herald the arrival of a woman seeking a cure to the rot nibbling at her limbs. Hannah even received a gilt-edged invitation from a duchess, asking her to call upon them with her basket of coloured glass. That visit resulted in a daughter being restored to full life, and a heavy sapphire was added to Hannah's hoard of the gemstones left behind when a soul was returned.

Through a process of trial and error, Hannah discovered that she needed a connection with an

Afflicted in order to identify the missing spark of a soul now contained in the glass. They would chat of inconsequential things much like any normal social visit, as Hannah sorted through the shards, seeking the one that resonated with her visitor's voice. A lump would form in her throat when a woman perched forward on the sofa with hands clasped and bright expectation on her face, only to meet with crushing disappointment.

"I'm sorry, it is not among these." Hannah's voice always caught on the words as she delivered the sad news.

One woman, the wife of an earl, became angry at being told her spark did not dwell within the basket.

"I shall take another. That red one is pretty and matches my gown. Give it to me at once," she demanded, and gestured with a gloved hand.

Hannah tucked the basket closer to her body and glanced at her husband. "I cannot. It does not work like that. I will not place another woman's soul in your body."

Her incensed ladyship rose to her feet. "Do you know who I am? I demand you cure me of this dreadful curse."

Wycliff pushed off from the window, where he had been a silent observer. "Do *you* know whom you are dealing with?" he asked in a quiet tone. His features shimmered as the hellhound dropped over him, and the large hound of Anubis sat in the middle of the parlour. The creature bared its long fangs and smoky, red-tipped fur drifted to a disturbance in the air.

The countess gasped and clutched the necklace at her throat, though whether to defend her jugular or the jewellery wasn't entirely clear. Behind the thin mask concealing her rotting features, wide eyes stared at Hannah. "What is that thing?"

"*That* is the creature who enables me to hunt down and return the missing souls taken from the Afflicted. I am sure our next foray to the afterlife will reveal the shard needed to stop the decay spreading through your limbs." Hannah kept a serious expression on her face. She suspected Wycliff relished the rumours that sprouted about him, and he secretly enjoyed shocking people when they glimpsed the hound. For a man who had once buried his secret deep, he now shared it freely.

Gossip had erupted in London that the viscount was a creature from Hell, and if society had been afraid of him before, it was nothing to how they felt now. Although it must be said that many people weren't that surprised by the news, given his reputation. For the common people, it somewhat allayed their fears knowing that Black Shuck stalked London solely to find foul souls and drag them back to where they belonged, not to feed on any of their number out after nightfall.

Having made his point that they would not be intimidated or threatened, Wycliff shrugged off his underworld persona and walked to Hannah's side. He took the basket from her and held it close to his chest.

"Now that I have made your acquaintance, it will be easier for me to find your missing spark. I am sure your next visit here will bring good news. Is a delay of a few days so terrible to bear, when it will result in immortality?" Hannah murmured as she stood next to her husband.

Hearing a person's voice and being in their presence would help guide Hannah's search on her next trip to the underworld. Rarely had she failed to find their spark after meeting with someone, and their second encounter was more joyous. A week later, even the rude countess was reunited with the missing piece of her soul. Not too surprisingly, she declined to have her heart weighed in the scales of Ma'at and chose to remain as one of the undead.

Life transformed in many ways for the unusual family in Westbourne Green. Joy flowed through Hannah that her body had thrown off the curse, and she could now dare to dream of what the future might hold for her and Wycliff. Her mother created an uproar by claiming a spot on the mage council, as England's only shadow mage. Not to mention the very public walk she had taken through London to the palace for a tête-à-tête with Queen Charlotte. The newspapers were filled with tales of the cured Afflicted, and the fear that had once roared through the streets crept back into the shadows.

Even Unwin and Alder took the decline in their clientele with good grace, although Wycliff muttered they had probably already spotted a new market in the range of services they offered to Unnaturals. As more creatures stepped into the light, they had particular needs that required the discreet help of Unwin and Alder.

Lord Tomlin retreated from London to a remote estate near the Scottish border. He claimed he wished to immerse himself in scholarly pursuits. Seraphina chuckled, certain that his fear fuelled his desperate search for a way to escape death itself.

Hannah's mother and husband conspired to find a way to navigate the dark path. One night, Wycliff's hellhound walked through all of Tomlin's protective wards and appeared at the foot of his bed. The hound reminded the mage that the jaws of Ammit, Devourer of the Dead, awaited him.

However, a shred of charity for the mage remained inside Hannah, for his magic flowed through Timmy's veins and gave the lad his gift. There was a chance, however remote, that Lord

Tomlin would use his time to make amends for his past actions.

Hannah's past actions paid dividends in her new life. Wycliff had engaged a solicitor to visit jewellers around London and farther afield in Europe, as they sought the best price for the gems that were their payment for services given to Anubis and Anput. The couple didn't want to ignite rumours by selling off the lot openly, but over a period of three months, enough jewels were sold to generate a life-changing sum.

In trying to decide how best to apply their newfound wealth, Hannah found a mentor in Lady Loburn. Her mother's best friend dispensed practical advice as they marshalled their resources in a plan of action. Seraphina and Hannah called on her to finalise several details before they all departed for their country homes to hunker down for the winter.

Lady Loburn embraced her friend. "I never tire of seeing your face. How I have missed you."

"Or more likely, missed our mischief," Seraphina murmured.

"That, too. I am so looking forward to next season. We shall be the gossiping matrons as our daughters make their mark." Kitty bent her head close to Seraphina's as the women plotted.

Hannah rang for tea and laid out her notes on the table. Once the older women had caught up,

Lady Loburn joined Hannah to review her progress. She wrote notes in the margin of a list and other items were struck through with a bold hand. "Excellent, Hannah, not a single pointless trapping on your list. It sounds as though you have a housekeeper to handle the day-to-day running of the household, and the handful of staff you have engaged so far will be enough to get by for now. Most of your house is still closed up, and I imagine it will only be yourself and Wycliff in residence throughout the year."

"Mrs Rossett is exceptionally capable, although getting on somewhat in years." The housekeeper had beamed at seeing Mireworth revived and had rubbed her hands at the prospect of more staff.

"Look for a sensible maid with potential, who can be trained up for the position one day," Lady Loburn said.

"Sensible ones seem light on the ground." Hannah pondered how Mary had come to work for their family. She would never have been engaged if *sensible* had been a criteria, but Hannah wouldn't trade her for any maid to be found in London.

"What about a butler?" Every grand home possessed an equally grand butler to cast a critical eye over its guests.

Lady Loburn scoffed. "There's no point in engaging a butler yet. Knowing you and Wycliff, I doubt you will entertain much. Besides, a butler is a critical position in a household and you must find the right one. Take your time to ensure a good fit. If you don't get along, he could make your life miserable."

"Or we will make him miserable. Not everyone is open-minded enough to accept Frank and Barnes." Hannah had determined that having the disembodied hand scuttle past while conducting interviews was a sure way to narrow down the number of candidates. Some maids fainted outright, others screamed. The few who stared with wide-eyed curiosity were hired on the spot.

"A married couple might provide a solution, if you can find a pair to take on both tasks." Lady Loburn moved on from the subject of staff to that of restoring and refurbishing Mireworth.

Lizzie was undertaking a similar task, although on a much grander scale, as she wrestled Harden's Mayfair mansion into shape and stamped her mark on its walls and floors. The two young women had spent many an hour discussing soft furnishings and the best colour combination to bring a room to life. Then, there were other, more *intimate* topics about their marriages they discussed in breathless whispers when completely alone.

The duke and duchess had already retired to Harden's country estate in Kent, and Hannah missed her friend terribly. Her mother had given each of them a small ensorcelled notebook with a pencil that cleverly hid down the spine, and an attached chain to make the book harder to lose. Now the friends always had a way to communicate close at hand. In the evening's quiet, they could catch up through short, chatty messages to one another that spanned the physical distance.

A few weeks later, the combined Miles and Wycliff family was almost ready to depart for Dorset.

"How many souls have you released now?" Seraphina asked over breakfast one morning. Hannah's mother sipped a cup of tea, relishing the taste after two years of dining only on *pickled cauliflower*.

"One hundred and thirty-two. I have twenty-seven crystals collected that do not belong to anyone who has yet crossed my path." Of those who had had their *ka* restored, less than fifty had availed themselves of the opportunity to have their heart weighed in Ma'at's balance. Hannah understood their reticence. She had thought that her own organ would tip the scales and couldn't look until Wycliff had murmured her worth against her ear. "We are still missing so many, and I've not even found half of the Afflicted that could have been created."

They had seized three hundred containers of infected face powder in the early days of the outbreak. Less than half that number of Afflicted were somewhat restored. In her mind, Hannah saw the souls trapped in shards of glass and hiding somewhere in Duat. She kept a ledger, tallying those who had been restored against those who continued to suffer in silence. A plan formulated in her mind to dig up those Afflicted they feared had been interred prematurely by their families. The question remained, though—would they still possess their minds after more than two years trapped in their coffins?

A sad smile flitted over Seraphina's face, and she patted her daughter's hand. "You do what you can, Hannah. We have turned back the tide of panic with the public announcement of those whose hearts have restarted. I have rather enjoyed my own return to court. There's nothing like regrowing one's legs to stimulate discussion. I think some people are jealous that the others like me may now be immortal."

The undead who no longer decayed had created a new species. They referred to themselves as *jewels*, both in reference to the crystal where the curse had imprisoned their spark, and to their enduring nature. Doctor Husom took a fatherly interest in their condition and made himself available to offer advice about how to withstand the centuries—should the women exist that long.

Another unexpected side effect was the lawyers, rubbing their hands with glee. So many rich nobles would need a way to financially sustain themselves through the years and protect their fortunes. Solicitors were drawing up plans and schemes to benefit the women, who could not legally hold property due to their dead status.

Hannah let out a sigh. There was so much to do, and so many demands on her time. How she looked forward to returning to Mireworth, where they planned to spend the winter. They had managed only two brief trips there in the preceding months, one to celebrate the autumn harvest, and another to view the progress of repairs to the roof and windows.

"You are right, Mother. We can do no more this year. Most nobles retired to their country homes months ago." Some only stayed to give Hannah time to find their spark. In spring, they would start anew. Besides, they could continue their search in Duat while nestled in the countryside. A trip to the underworld would be a pleasant way to escape the winter cold.

The next day, Wycliff cast around their bedroom one last time. "Are you all packed?"

"*I* am packed." Hannah stressed the pronoun.

Her husband rolled his eyes and muttered, "I don't know why you put up with that maid."

"Because she is loyal, honest, and excellent at her job. Although I do admit, she is rather distracted by planning her wedding to Frank."

Mary had expressed her desire to marry at Mireworth, where Frank had proposed. Hannah thought it a fine idea and just the opportunity they needed to bring a dose of happiness into the long neglected house. "How has Pike settled in?"

With the change in their finances, Wycliff had engaged a valet—the country born and bred Pike who had once served Lord Stoneleigh, before the latter's untimely demise to bloodthirsty puppets.

Wycliff picked up a battered leather satchel from the settee at the end of the bed. Within he placed a book to read on the journey, a notebook and pencil, and a pack of playing cards. "Exactly as we expected—the man hasn't batted an eye at either Frank or Barnes, and looked positively joyous when I said we were going to divide our time between London and Dorset."

"He ties a fine knot, too. Your cravats rival Papa's these days." Hannah's forefinger hovered over the perfectly tied knot.

A warm smile simmered in Wycliff's eyes as he held out his arm to her. "Ready?"

"Yes." The entire family would depart for Mireworth. Hannah and her mother were both keen to uncover the full story of Kemsit, the occupant of the tower, and de Cliffe, the man who had brought her there six hundred years before. They also had gardens to plan, as the mage would flex her gift to restore the grounds.

Only Cook would remain, as was her custom. To ensure the old woman wasn't alone over Christmas, her niece and her husband had moved into the house. The younger couple would undertake any tasks needed in the family's absence and would be responsible for tending to the chickens. Hannah's mind swirled as the couple had unloaded their luggage and never batted an eye at Barnes. The young man had a serious countenance, but intelligence glinted in his eyes and he asked thoughtful questions of Sir Hugh about the tasks to be performed.

"You wouldn't be thinking of poaching those two from your mother, would you, Hannah?" Seraphina murmured.

Hannah grinned. "Absolutely! They could be the perfect addition to our household and could grow into their roles as we do."

"I suppose that is the way of things in this family. I did steal Cook from her former employer. Not that Lord Branvale ever appreciated Rosie or the others. Although technically I didn't really steal them, since Branvale no longer needed them after he was murdered." Seraphina winked at Hannah, as Sir Hugh handed her up into their carriage.

"Mother! Tell me you didn't...?" Hannah stared after her mother, who cackled in laughter.

Wycliff took Hannah's arm. "I now understand

why your father has such broad shoulders...to carry all the trouble your mother causes."

Hannah stepped up into the carriage and settled her skirts around her. "Some days I don't know whether to believe Mother's tales or if she embellishes events to alarm me."

Wycliff sat next to her. "I imagine that if we are blessed with children one day, they will think the same of us, and that our stories of the Duat and dispatching souls will sound equally far-fetched."

That didn't ease Hannah's mind; rather, the opposite. Surely her mother's tales of outrageous antics couldn't possibly be even half true. Could they...?

2

———————

Two DAYS LATER, the carriages swept up the drive of Mireworth near the little village of Selham in Dorset. For only the second time since her acquaintance with the old house, Hannah would go in through the front door. She glanced at Wycliff from under her lashes, remembering the first time. He had swept her up into his arms and carried her across the threshold into the gloom—rather like Hades had carried Persephone to his dark domain. Just as that goddess had done, Hannah had grown to love her underworld hero and gladly divided her time between two realms.

Frank pulled the carriage to a halt under the portico. Peering out the window, Hannah marvelled at how great a difference a few small changes had made in the manor house. Lanterns on either side of the double front doors emitted a

15

welcoming golden light, and the steps were freshly swept of leaves, dirt, and seed heads. Weeds had been pulled from around the foundations of the house and the soil turned over, ready for spring planting. Seraphina had suggested lavender, for both its fragrance and because the soft purple flowers and silvery foliage would look marvellous against the creamy stone. Or they would, once the exterior layer of grime succumbed to the gentle cleaning spell the mage cast. Even now, patches were exposed, making the house's skin look some-what like that of a giraffe with its darker spots.

Wycliff's eyes burned with hope as he took Hannah's hand to help her down, and they walked toward the house.

The front door swung open to reveal Mrs Rossett's beaming face. "Welcome, Lord and Lady Wycliff. Do come inside out of the nasty weather. Looks like rain is right on your heels."

Hannah stepped inside and let out a sigh. Her mother had worked her magic and installed a type of heating she called *geothermal* under the ground floor of Mireworth, as she had at Westbourne Green. Pipes ran deep into the earth and with a few self-perpetuating spells, the mage funnelled warmth from the ground upward, dispersing it through grates set in the floorboards. The system was part magic, part genius, and pure bliss. Not only was Mireworth watertight, she was now dry and warm from her toes upward as the heat gently rose to the upper floors.

"Is the dining room completed, Mrs Rossett?" Hannah asked as she peeled off her warm outer layers. A new maid took the items and bobbed a curtsey before taking them away. There were a number of new faces among the staff, engaged in London and then dispatched to Mrs Rossett to settle in to the household.

The housekeeper winked. "It is, milady. Would you like to see it first?"

"Oh, yes, please." She linked arms with the housekeeper and they walked over the tiled representation of the Duat in the entry hall.

With more staff, the family could no longer dine in the cosy kitchen. But still Hannah refused to crack open the door to the cold, dark, formal dining room. Perhaps she could turn it into a laboratory one day, or a gloomy parlour for unwanted guests. Until then, she had selected a small room at the rear of the house that might once have been a study or private parlour, and declared it the family dining room. The room possessed glass doors that opened out to the side garden. Or it would, once her mother worked her magical green thumb in spring.

"It's wonderful!" Hannah exclaimed as she stepped within.

The redecoration of the space had occurred in

their absence. Hannah had picked a cheerful wall-paper in golden yellow, cream, and white. Large gold-flecked bumblebees buzzed between daisies the size of dinner plates. The table could seat eight and was of a size to be practical, but not so vast as to be intimidating if only Hannah and Wycliff were in residence. The chairs were upholstered in a sunny yellow and cream stripe that comple-mented the wallpaper. A fire blazed in the hearth, and the lamps cast a soft yellow light. A thick rug in mossy green covered the glossy floorboards. Over-all, the room conjured the warmth of a summer's day.

"Room by room, Mireworth is coming back to life." Mrs Rossett beamed, delighted to a have family in the rooms above and staff to boss around in her kitchen.

"I cannot wait to see what else has changed." Hannah would miss the kitchen table, but the new family rooms would create their own memories over the coming years. She could imagine hot summers where they could fling open the doors and admire the garden and perhaps a flow of friends and family as they sank their roots deeper into the community.

"There is something I would show you, Hannah, upstairs." Wycliff held out his hand to her.

At the sound of the second carriage outside,

Mrs Rossett said, "I'll show Sir Hugh and Lady Miles to their rooms. Then I'll crack the whip and have supper ready for you all, once you are settled." Mrs Rossett bustled back to the entrance hall to take charge of directing Hannah's parents to their rooms.

At the top of the stairs, Hannah's parents went in one direction and she and Wycliff took another. They stopped outside the dark panelled door that led to Lady Wycliff's suite.

Wycliff took a strip of blue silk from his pocket and tied it around Hannah's eyes. "Can you see anything?" he whispered by her ear.

"No. Is this necessary?" A tremble of excitement ran through her limbs. Whatever had he organised?

"Yes. I wanted this to be a surprise, though if you do not like it, you can change it." Doubt crept into his voice.

Hannah reached out and found his hands, clasping them in hers. "Show me this surprise before you prejudge that I might not like it. Besides, you will have put care into whatever it is, and that alone endears it to me."

The latch clicked as he opened the door, and a waft of linseed oil drifted past her nose. Wycliff took her hand and placed the other on her waist to guide her into the room. Hard floorboards under her shoes turned to the softness of a rug. Warmth washed over her body as they stopped, and she guessed she stood before the lighted fire.

The blindfold fell away, and she blinked for a moment. Outside, darkness rolled across the land early with the arrival of winter. But before her, cheerful flames banished the cold and gloom. Then, her eyes roamed over the wall, where someone had painted a *tromp l'oeil*. To one side of the fireplace stood tall trees with gnarled bark. Their branches spread along the top of the wall and a few poked onto the ceiling and adjoining wall. Lush ferns nestled at their feet. To the other side of the fireplace lay a rounded patch of bright green grass. A stream flowed past, the water bubbling over smooth stones. In a beam of sunlight stood a peacock with his tail spread. The artist had used metallic paints to make the feathers iridescent. Two peahens sat nearby and appeared to be chatting and ignoring the vain male.

Words stuttered in her throat at the marvellous scene. "Oh, Wycliff. It's the glade at Westbourne Green."

"I wanted you to have something of your home here." His voice came from behind her.

"It's beautiful." The more she studied the painting, the more delightful small details she found. From the sparrows and finches flitting in the trees, to the golden fish leaping in the water. A faint rustle swept across the leaves and ruffled the peacock's feathers.

Hannah gasped. "It moved."

Wycliff's attention remained fixed on her reaction. "The local aftermage artist painted it and infused it with a slight movement."

Tears misted her eyes. "Thank you. But you did not have to do this. Mireworth is my home."

He grinned, and her heart melted a little more. "I wanted to do something to mark the occasion. You will have plenty of opportunity to make the rest of the suite to your taste. The furnishings are temporary, until you decide what style you would like."

Only now did she turn to survey the rest of her room. It had a mismatched and haphazard appearance. The large bed possessed ornate barley twists on each corner post, but its canopy was empty, bereft of the heavy fabric that had once draped the bed to keep out the drafts. The coverlet was made of floral fabric in light pinks and creams that clashed with the heavy earth tones of the drapes on the windows. The rugs scattered over the floor were a mix of swirls and lines and a rainbow of colours. Even the furniture couldn't decide what time period or fashion it wanted to follow. The heavy bed was from centuries ago, but a delicate painted writing desk that could only be Georgian sat beneath a window. Two tall armoires of polished walnut and inlaid ebony stood guard on either side of a boxy dressing table, a plain stool before it with a yellow-and-red-striped cushion.

"I rather like it. It gives the room character." The room would be primarily her dressing room and private retreat, in any case. Her nights would be spent in Wycliff's adjoining room. Bit by bit, they revived the rooms they would need and use. Many would remain closed, once any pressing damage was repaired, as there was no point in being frivolous with their money.

Wycliff wrapped his arms around her and pulled her close. A sigh heaved through his chest. "None of this would have been possible without you. You, Hannah, are a miracle."

An hour later, they joined Hannah's parents in the new dining room. Their footman, Victor Mason, had been acquired in London and dispatched to Mireworth. He entered the room carrying dishes, accompanied by Mrs Rossett and Hollie Bennet, a young maid from a nearby village. An attack of nerves worked its way through Hannah. While they employed only a modest staff totalling ten, it seemed an enormous number of people to have under her charge.

"You have outdone yourself, Mrs Rossett," Hannah said as the lids were removed from the serving dishes.

The housekeeper clasped her hands together.

"I am quite enjoying myself as things get back to how they used to be years ago."

"Christmas will be rather special this year." Not since she was a child had Hannah anticipated the festive season this much.

"Now, where has that Barnes got to? He can assist me in the kitchen if he's free." Mrs Rossett glanced around the room.

The hand scuttled out from under the table and sat obediently at the older woman's feet. Then he tapped her shoe to attract her attention when she failed to notice him.

"Ah. There you are, my helping hand." She scooped him up and placed him on an empty serving tray. "I shall leave you all in the capable hands of Mason." She nodded to the footman stationed by the buffet, and left carrying Barnes and trailed by Hollie.

Dinner passed with subdued conversation, everyone tired after two days of travel. While Mason gathered up the dishes, the family retired to the drawing room, where once Seraphina and Sir Hugh had made their impromptu bedroom. Like Hannah's suite upstairs, an eclectic mix of furniture and furnishings had been rustled up for the space. Sheba the spaniel flopped herself upon the rug in front of the fire and was snoring in less than a minute.

Hannah curled her feet up under her to read in

an oversized armchair covered in blue velvet brocade. Wycliff and her father set up the chessboard on a round table between two leather Chesterfield armchairs. Seraphina carried a box to the writing desk to review her correspondence.

After an hour of quiet companionship, they all rose to seek their beds. Wycliff scooped up the spaniel and carried her upstairs. Her parents walked arm in arm, their heads bent together. Mary waited for Hannah in her room, and she took a seat at the dressing table. The maid stifled a yawn as she pulled the pins from Hannah's hair. They were all keen to climb into bed for a solid night's sleep.

"Leave it loose." Hannah waved Mary's hands away when she reached to braid it. Wycliff would undo any plait, and Hannah suspected sleep wouldn't be on her husband's mind in any case. Hannah slipped into her nightgown and shrugged the robe around her shoulders. "Good night, Mary. I shall see you in the morning."

"Good night, milady." Mary placed the guard in front of the fire and then headed for her own bed.

Hannah padded on bare feet through the connecting door to Wycliff's room. She found it in darkness, apart from the flicker of the fire. Her husband stood with one hand on the mantel, staring into the flames.

"Mistress of Mireworth," he murmured against

the sensitive skin of her neck as he pulled her into his arms.

Hannah didn't think she would ever tire of being called that, but there was one slight adjustment she would make. Mistress of Mireworth's mysteries. Yes, much better.

3

THE NEXT MORNING, the family assembled in the daisy garden room (as Hannah had begun to call it in her mind) for breakfast. The temperature continued to drop outside, but inside was toasty warm thanks to the fire in the hearth, and the heated air wafting through the ornate brass plate set in the floor. Barnes sat over the metal grate while Sheba stretched out on the rug in front of the fire.

"You should have been an architect, Lady Miles. These ducts are remarkable," Wycliff said as he poured coffee.

"In another life, perhaps. I enjoy the sort of designing that buildings and gardens require. When it comes to keeping fingers and toes warmed, it helps to be a mage with a close relationship to Mother Nature. She allows me to position the piping where it needs to be and sends the warmth up through it." Seraphina selected a piece of toast and centred it on her plate.

"I intend to launch a campaign to find any secrets Mireworth is hiding, with Barnes as my co-explorer, if he is agreeable?" Hannah glanced at the hand, who had flopped over onto his back on the grate. He raised a thumb, which she took as agreement. Then all his fingers went loose, rather like the dog rolling in the grass after a long walk.

To marshal her resources and keep track of their efforts, Hannah utilised a copy of the house plans they had been using to organise the restoration work. On a previous visit, Hannah and Wycliff had ventured into every single room and assessed the damage. Each room was then assigned a colour to denote the type of work required, and the space was shaded in on the plans. Rooms shaded in red needed substantial work, orange minor repairs, and green needed only redecoration. Their travels through the house revealed the red areas were confined to one side, where it then bled out into orange and faded to green. On the same set of colourful plans, Hannah pencilled in what she considered to be the most likely places for any previous Lord Wycliff to have hidden journals or letters.

Wycliff looked up from the newspaper. "If I might suggest a starting point—there is a safe in our bedroom, tucked behind a panel in the wall. It is locked, but I never bothered to look for a key, as my father would have sold anything of value. However, the vague possibility exists that it could contain papers."

"I can see to the safe. It's been years since I coaxed open a lock." Seraphina's eyes sparkled with mischief, and Hugh snorted into his coffee.

There were days when Hannah wondered what exactly her parents had got up to when they were her age. Should she be out causing scandal and mischief? That sounded rather tiring when she had so much to do already. In addition, she walked the living realm on behalf of two goddesses from the underworld. Even if she had the inclination, when would she have time for getting herself into trouble?

After breakfast, Wycliff led the way up the stairs and along the hall to the suites occupied by the lord and lady of Mireworth. They had a corner of the house (thankfully in an area shaded green on the map, with no structural damage) where once the windows had looked over the expansive gardens. Now they surveyed a wilderness with its own sort of untamed beauty.

In the oversized room he shared with Hannah, Wycliff crossed to the wall holding two armoires. He dug his fingernails under the trim of the chair rail and pulled. A panel popped open at chest height, perfectly blended with the striped wallpaper, and revealed a solid black metal door with a brass keyhole.

Hannah's father let out a low whistle. "What treasure might await us? All the answers to our questions could be trapped inside."

Seraphina rubbed her hands together and blew on them. Then she reached out and laid a hand flat on the safe. With one finger, she stroked the metal beside the keyhole. After a few seconds a loud *thunk* sounded, and the door jutted open an inch. She stepped back and waved Wycliff forward.

"Thank you," Wycliff murmured as he pulled the door open.

Hannah peered around him, wondering what would be inside. The space appeared inky black. Certainly no bundles of papers or hidden journals lay within. As Wycliff had observed earlier, it appeared to be empty. Then he reached in and extracted an object that hadn't been immediately obvious because of its dark colour.

A gasp surged up Hannah's throat as she recognised the shape and type of box. What woman wouldn't? Her husband held a black velvet jewel case. And a rather large one at that, the top embossed with the golden logo of a legendary London jeweller.

He met Hannah's stare with a dark one that burned with hope. A lump bobbed up and down his throat before he could speak. "It's the Wycliff diamonds. I thought they were sold off years ago, even before Mother died. I'm struggling to recollect the last time she wore them. A Christmas dinner, I think, when I was no more than ten."

An ornate brass catch held the box closed. Wycliff slid a finger under it and flicked it free. Then he raised the lid. Hannah and Seraphina leaned closer, expecting to exclaim over a diamond necklace, matching earrings, a bracelet, and perhaps even a tiara to complete the set. Except their eyes fell upon...a piece of paper.

Someone had cut out a circular shape and laid it in the gap for the jewels.

Wycliff lifted the paper. Underneath were scattered pebbles to replicate the weight of the jewellery. His shoulders sagged, and he slammed the box closed. He stalked to the bed and dropped down upon it. With his head bowed, he clutched the case in his long fingers.

Hannah glanced at her parents and tilted her head toward the door. Seraphina squeezed Hannah's upper arm and left on silent feet with Hugh, closing the door behind them. Hannah walked over to her husband and considered what to say. Disappointment rolled through her, even though she had no memory of the Wycliff family jewels, nor had she expected to discover such a treasure. What must he be suffering, to have hope flare into life inside him, only to be dashed one more time?

She sat next to him and tugged one hand away from the case to clasp it in both her own.

"I am a fool," he murmured.

"Why?" She lifted his arm around her and nestled her head on his shoulder.

"For one brief moment, I allowed myself to believe my father had actually left something of worth in his wake. Then, as quickly as that dream flared into brilliant life, it crumbled into dust. I should have known. Nothing but disappointment ever came from that quarter." He lifted the lid on the case and stared within.

It had a raised centrepiece to allow the necklace to drape around an artificial neck. A small curve might have contained a bracelet. Two slots in the middle were for earrings. Someone had pressed a cut-out drawing into the larger shape. Only charcoal lines and swirls hinted at what had been lost. The necklace had had an unusual design, the central drop like a flower bloom, supported by a twist of leaves.

"As a young woman, my mother had many suitors who laid titles, grand estates, and jewels at her feet," she said softly. "Despite the wealth dangled before her, she chose my father. The penniless surgeon who grew potatoes in his attic room." Hannah never grew tired of the tale about how her parents had met and fallen in love. Other women might prefer their fairy tales with princes and dashing white stallions. Hannah adored the story of an honest man who loved with every piece of him and the woman who had seen—and still saw —the real treasure before her.

A sigh heaved through Wycliff's tall frame. "I am doubly a fool, for thinking my father might have left an expensive parure in the safe, when it would have bought him a few more weeks at the gaming table. And twice a fool for forgetting that you would prefer a stack of books over a spray of diamonds around your neck. The vain part of me seized on the chance to give you something beautiful."

"How many times do I have to remind you that you have already given me the most amazing gift? Your heart." She placed her hand on his cheek and turned his face to hers. Then she kissed him.

RAIN KEPT them inside that day, so Hannah marked off Wycliff's bedroom as having been searched with a big red X. Then, she and Barnes embarked on their investigation with the next room in her sights. In making a list of likely hiding places, Hannah thought the older rooms might conceal holes where documents could be secreted. When

Wycliff's ancestor had built the current house, instead of starting with a clear paddock, he had incorporated whatever building already stood on the spot. Hence the formal dining room had clear Tudor origins in its low ceiling and age-stained exposed beams. Then, of course, the tower had stood guard since the twelfth century.

"We begin our search in the horrid formal dining room, Barnes," Hannah said to the hand as they walked the hall. Part of her wanted the examination of that room over and done with so she could shut the door and possibly seal it up, never to be opened again.

The thought made her pause. What about the room conjured such a reaction? She delighted in all of Mireworth's rooms, except that one. Perhaps a ghost lingered in a corner and cast the evil eye at her. She would call forth her underworld form and dispatch it, if that were the case.

Hannah pushed open the heavy walnut doors, the timber aged to black. Cast-iron hinges with long curves jutted across the wood and seemed ridiculously large for their job. The rain-laden clouds outside the house barely allowed any light to penetrate the thick glass of the window and what little did struggled to filter through and cast watery shapes on the floor. She held the small glow mushroom in front of her to light the way to the room's single lantern.

Her mother had created numerous glow lamps to illuminate the dark corners and banish the gloom from Mireworth's halls and rooms. They first placed them on the frequented routes and where they would be most useful for staff in the dark and narrow servants' corridors. The disused dining room warranted only one lamp, squatting on the table and looking like an ugly gnome hugging its knees to its chest.

Hannah tapped the light to activate it and turned in a slow circle. A shudder worked its way down her spine. She had ventured into every room, cupboard, and corridor with Wycliff to take note of damage and needed repairs, but the unscathed dining room remained a mystery, as well as her least favourite place in the entire house. Quite frankly, she didn't like it one bit. Nor could she come up with a reason why both her body and mind skittered from it. She had been in some lovely old Tudor pubs that exuded warmth and charm. Sadly, none of that was to be found here.

Perhaps her opinion would change if they lit the large fire and placed lights all around? Burning a sweet-smelling wood would remove the dusty odour, and the company of good friends would also enliven the atmosphere. *No. I still won't spend any longer than absolutely necessary in here*, a voice in the back of her mind murmured.

"Where shall we start, Barnes? You pick a

corner and we'll work around from there." Hannah carried a smaller glow lamp with her. Shadows moved deeper into the recesses as they passed. She hoped there weren't any large spiders that might leap out and challenge Barnes to battle.

The hand pointed to the corner to the left of the fireplace and began his search. He tapped and poked the floorboards, skirting, and wall. Hannah performed the same process at a higher level. Inch by inch, they shuffled along the wall toward the fireplace. The ornately carved fire surround received extra attention. Hannah pressed the centre of every rose and ran a finger along every leaf. Part of her hoped to trigger a secret latch and a creak that would herald a panel swinging open to reveal a hoard of journals recording the full and uncensored history of the house.

No such luck.

On the other side of the fireplace, they continued their slow progress to the next corner. At which point Hannah arched her back and inadvertently made eye contact with a large spider regarding her from above.

"Time for a break, Barnes. What do you think?" Hannah's throat scratched from the dusty air, and she longed for a hot cup of tea.

Barnes gave the thumbs up. They were walking across the floor when the hand tripped on a knot and tumbled to one side. He crawled back to the offending gap that had caught his finger, and froze. Then he crooked his finger at Hannah and pointed to the hole.

"What have you found?" Hannah knelt on the floorboards, which were rough and hand hewn. No two were exactly the same in either size or appearance. Decades of feet had worn their surfaces smooth, but knot holes and gaps remained.

Barnes gestured to the hole again and placed his knuckle close to it as though he peered through.

"I think it is merely a defect in the wood." The short plank had a gap large enough for her to fit in her finger up to the first joint, which was what had tripped Barnes on his way past. When she wriggled her finger in the hole, the length of wood creaked in protest. "I say, this bit seems loose."

Hannah angled her finger and pulled. The plank shuddered but held. Hmm...maybe it wasn't as loose as it seemed? Barnes tapped her hand, and she slipped her finger out. The hand wedged his thicker finger in. Then he walked backward. Hannah wasn't sure his plan would work. Grabbing on to his idea, though, Hannah used both her hands to clutch the waving wrist. She leaned back and hauled on Barnes, who held fast to the plank.

With a pop, she tumbled backward still clutching Barnes, now attached to a piece of floorboard. The hand's finger was wedged into the knothole and the plank covered him like a roof.

"Well done!" Hannah took hold of the piece of wood while Barnes struggled to remove his digit. It took a bit of teamwork, but once he was free, Hannah turned to their discovery. She lowered the glow mushroom and found a narrow gap under the floorboard.

And an aged journal with the pages curled up from damp.

"Oh, brilliant, Barnes." Hannah crossed her legs and Barnes perched on her knee. She handed him the small lamp, which he held out to act as a reading light.

The leather on the front of the journal cracked and split as she levered it open. Some of the pages were stuck together, and the ink was smeared from damp and mould. "We might not find anything useful in here."

The unknown author had a large and open hand. As Hannah read snatches here and there, her mind grasped the difference between their current way of speaking and the odd and old-fashioned turns of phrase. Some of the words were irretrievable, lost on the mould-ridden page. Others leapt out at her with a horrible clarity.

A witch hath been spawned in Selham...

Her heart sank and her breath turned to ash in her throat. She closed the journal and held it shut, as though she hoped to erase the hideous event from history.

Hannah climbed to her feet and lifted the lantern from Barnes. "I cannot read it in here." A chill washed over her skin, despite the warmth seeping up through the pipes deep in the earth. She glanced into the corners, expecting the tragic babe's ghost to crawl across the floor.

As they left the room and she tugged the doors shut, unshed tears misted her vision. Had a mother long ago hidden her child, knowing the mage council would not allow her to live? Or had the woman surrendered her daughter, believing what men preached—that a woman's body was an inadequate vessel for power?

She headed for the sunny dining room, needing its bright charm to dispel the shadows gathering in her mind. On the way, Hannah passed Hollie. "Could you fetch me a pot of tea, please?" Barnes tugged on the hem of Hannah's skirt and pointed to the maid. Hannah added together the clues. "Could you take Barnes to the kitchen with you? I suspect he wants to assist Mrs Rossett, since I have called an end to our search for today."

"Of course, milady." The maid scooped up Barnes and carried him in her open palms, where he sighted the way as though he stood on deck once more.

In the dining room, a chair was positioned by the terrace doors and caught a few rays of watery sunlight. Hannah sat and gazed at the journal.

Drawing a deep sigh, she cracked open the protesting leather. She squinted and scanned the lines, trying to discern the fate of the child from three hundred years ago. Bits didn't make sense. The ink had long ago dribbled off the page. But a line grabbed her attention.

By a small mercy, the demon had already passed by the time the mage council's man arrived.

A trickle of relief eased the pain in Hannah's chest. At least Wycliff's ancestor had not been a party to the infanticide of girl mages. A tragedy for the mother, no doubt wracked by anxiety over the fate of her daughter, only to have her snatched away by any of the common illnesses that struck children.

It is our burden to bear, because of the witch who once walked this land. Will we never remove her stain?

A snort escaped her at that sentence. Kemsit was no more a burden or stain than Hannah's mother. She suspected the mage council's abhorrent treatment of girls haunted them, and their guilt and mistaken beliefs festered into their monstrous imaginings about women mages. Imagine how much richer and different their world might be, if all mage children were treated equally and given the same chance to find their way in the world.

4

HANNAH FOUND Wycliff in his reclaimed study. The stack of crates remained in the corner, waiting for the rooms above to be repaired and refurbished before the small items were returned to shelves and side tables. He sat at the desk, a pile of invoices before him, as he worked on the estate accounts. Rain pounded the glass at his back, but no water gained entry due to the new pane in one corner.

He glanced up, and a smile eased the tight lines in his face. With one hand he returned the pen to its holder, the other he extended to her. "You look worried," he said.

Wycliff slid an arm around her waist as she leaned into his side. "I am no more worried than you. How do the finances hold?"

They had discussed expenses at length, weighing every purchase before they committed their money to any project or item. Their frugality would bear fruit in the coming years, setting the estate to rights and benefiting the entire community as they all flourished.

"We are on track, and thankfully none of the builders have cost much over what we budgeted. What have you discovered?" He gestured to the journal.

She placed the battered book on the desk before him. "A journal from the fifteen hundreds. Barnes found it quite by accident when he tripped in a knothole. Many of the pages are ruined by mould and damp after three hundred years beneath the floor, but I managed to decipher a few sentences within."

"Oh?" Wycliff placed a finger under the cover and several pages stuck to the leather and turned as one.

"It mentions a witch spawned in the village." Her voice rasped over the words.

His hand tightened at her waist. "A girl mage."

"Yes. Then further, the author writes that the child died before the mage council's man arrived. Why did your ancestors have such a dim view of women mages?" She narrowed her gaze, wishing his ancestors would appear for questioning. Were they simply perpetuating misogynist views that were commonly held in earlier times, or had some unfortunate event shaped their opinions?

His fingers drummed a beat on the desk's green leather blotter. "Some prejudices are deeply ingrained, and passed down with each generation, like a tendency to weak chins. My father influenced my early opinions and that coloured how I viewed the Afflicted and your mother. It takes time and effort to set aside what you are led to believe from a young age, and to discover the truth for yourself."

She managed a sad smile. To her, the phrase *a witch hath been spawned* conveyed so much about the mistreatment and misunderstanding of powerful women, and all Unnatural creatures, through the millennia. Only a handful of years had passed since the Unnaturals Act had given those individuals the same rights as every Englishman.

"We cannot change the past, but we can build a better future." How she wished she could travel back in time and save all those children, but at least she could play her part to ensure history did not repeat itself.

Wycliff placed a swift kiss on her lips. "Perhaps the next hole Barnes falls into will be deeper, and he'll dig out something from before Tudor times that will shed some light on Kemsit's history here."

That made humour ripple through her and dispelled the sombre mood. "Perhaps. We will try again tomorrow. Now that the rain has eased, after lunch I might go for a walk outside to clear my head."

On her large map, Hannah marked the Tudor dining room with a red X and the number two. Down the margin of the map she listed the numbers' significance. Wycliff's bedroom bore a one, and a note about the safe and empty necklace case. Beside the number two she noted the Tudor era journal they'd found. A few rooms were already marked with an X. The refurbished dining room, the kitchen, servants' dining hall, and the study had been eliminated easily. One by one, the red crosses would proliferate across the map until she reached the end of her journey. At that point, Hannah hoped, their curiosity would be satisfied about the history of the house and of Kemsit.

After the midday meal, Hannah sought the escape of the skeletal garden. The cold air flushed her cheeks, and she hugged a warm pelisse around her body. Ideas swirled in her head, and the quiet of the desolate garden allowed her to sort through them and determine a direction.

As she always did when unsure how to proceed, she started right back at the very beginning—Lizzie's engagement ball. A nagging suspicion whispered that everything was connected and there were no coincidences. Some force had guided Seraphina to have Wycliff invited to the ball, so that he and Hannah crossed paths. What if the hand nudging them onto a collision course had been that of Kemsit?

If Hannah pursued that line of thought, it implied the shadow mage had kept one wary eye on the descendants of de Cliffe over the centuries. Perhaps the shadow mage had intended that one day, an heir of de Cliffe's would meet the child of a fellow shadow mage? How she wished Kemsit had remained in the Duat, where they might have conversed with her and learned the true tale. Instead, they had to find what puzzle pieces they could and determine how they all fit together.

Along an overgrown path between unruly yews, Hannah explored the wintry landscape. Once the trees shook off their leaves and delicate summer perennials hibernated back in the earth, gardens revealed their structure and bones. Her mother declared the grounds well laid out, with little needed in the way of alteration. She did intend to enlarge the pond so that they could row upon it in summertime, and she planned a new garden with heady scents for the space beside the new dining room.

As she turned a corner, Hannah stared up at Mireworth. At one end, the round pink tower sat enclosed in a square prison. How she longed to pull down the outer stone and reveal it once more. If they peeled back the entire enclosure to ground level, the tower would be a stunning feature. The symmetry of the house was slightly off kilter because of the odd tower, but its lines would make sense once the medieval structure was unveiled to the world again.

She pushed along a path littered with leaves and twigs. A ragged hole in a hedge revealed a circular lawn with two benches set opposite each other. Hannah chose one stone seat in the watery sunlight. There was much to organise as December marched on. Frank and Mary would wed on Christmas Eve, and Hannah wanted to make it a magical and intimate affair for the couple. There was also the issue of where they would live. Frank didn't enjoy being stuck in the house, but a lady's maid was supposed to be available when her mistress needed her—not living out in the stables. But how to reconcile what they all required? As Lady Wycliff, Hannah could simply dictate that Mary sleep in a room in the house. But she would never do that. No, there would be a solution that made all parties content. She had only to figure it out.

Her mind flew in a hundred different directions, but couldn't resolve a single problem. She rose to continue walking, hoping the activity would ease her frustration. As she paced the overgrown paths, Hannah considered how Kemsit's influence flowed through the house. Only the shadow mage could have conjured the tiled representation of the

Duat hundreds of years after she retired from the living realm. Perhaps she had also influenced the decision to cast the goddess of justice in bronze for the conservatory pool. Were there other echoes of Kemsit to be found on the grounds, if one looked with the right eyes?

With a gloved hand, Hannah rubbed the spot at the base of her throat where Anput's ankh lay under her skin. Her underworld form enveloped her, and enabled her to see souls and shades lingering in the world of the living. She scanned the tangled trees and borders, but not a single ghost prowled the derelict grounds in winter. Then a burst of laughter made Hannah turn down one particular pathway.

Up ahead, on a bare patch of lawn, two figures shimmered. Hannah caught only wisps of their outlines, like silver fish darting far below the water's surface. One shade seemed to be chasing the other. Then, they stopped and their forms filled in a little more, as though drawn by an artist with a quick hand and a charcoal stick.

A woman with long black hair and a swirling green cloak.

A broad man bundled in shaggy brown furs.

Snow appeared under their feet.

The man scooped up a handful of snow and formed it into a ball. His image became more solid as he worked, until he resembled what some called a ghost. He threw the ball at the woman, who laughed in delight. She raised her hands and a flurry of balls rose from the ground and pelted the man, bombarding him with a wall of snow.

Kemsit.

Hannah stood frozen to the spot, not wanting to lose the scene playing out before her. Her hands clasped the ankh, made corporeal in her afterlife guise.

The man, who must have been de Cliffe, lifted his hands in defeat. "I surrender!" His voice echoed around the space and bounced off the wild and untrimmed hedges. His shade hovered above the ground and he trod air toward Kemsit. Then he swept a courtly bow. "What does my lady command of her servant?"

"To my tower." She pointed in its direction.

As Hannah stared at Mireworth, a lump caught in her throat. As the unseen artist redrew the picture, the tower broke free of its prison and the stone glowed a soft pink. It abutted an ancient-looking fortress, rather than the current Georgian house. For one marvellous moment, Hannah saw the original castle to which de Cliffe had brought the Egyptian mage, the brooding fortification soft-ened by the tower nestled beside it. Then the illu-sion faded, and the current form of Mireworth reappeared.

De Cliffe picked up a laughing Kemsit and

carried her in ghostly arms. As the couple drew near to Hannah, the echo of the mage's soul met Hannah's gaze. "The tower," she repeated, before the two figures disappeared into the mist.

The tower. It has to be a message reaching through time. Hannah's attention remained on the tower as she headed back to the house. The brief echo she'd seen of Kemsit and de Cliffe confirmed the theory she had been pondering about the two.

"They were happy," Hannah murmured to herself as she released her Duat form. More than happy. Kemsit had the glow of a woman in love. But how long had the couple spent in each other's company, if the mage council had been determined to erase her from English soil?

"Their secret is here somewhere. I have only to find it." A splatter of rain landed on her face, and Hannah hurried inside.

HANNAH GLANCED into the drawing room, but found no sign of her mother. Even her father was absent, despite the frigid temperature. The doctor had slipped into the routine of doing rounds and had made himself available to anyone in the village who required his help. Timmy accompanied him and the lad's confidence in his abilities grew.

"Up," Hannah muttered to herself, and headed for the secret passageway to the tower.

Over the preceding months, they had made access easier. A careful study of the house plans revealed the bedrooms between and around which the tunnel skirted. Armed with that knowledge, they created a doorway in the back wall of a room and through to the trapped tower beyond. While not a perfect solution, it meant no more bending over to walk down the original cramped corridor where Wycliff had explored as a child.

Up the spiral Hannah went, to find her mother reclining on a chaise in what little sunlight the day could muster. Bringing furniture up the tight spiral had caused no small amount of cursing from the men, but both women appreciated their efforts. Now, Kemsit's tower had come back to life and was once more a lady's solar.

Hannah had chosen rugs in bold red and deep green to cover the floor. Two chaises sat at an angle to each other, with a small occasional table between them. She had layered colour and texture in the turret room. Enormous cushions featuring cranes with outstretched wings were piled on the floor before the fire, large enough that Hannah could flop on them to read.

"I saw them!" Hannah announced as she crossed the lush rugs. She seated herself on a chaise, perching on the edge to talk to her mother.

"Who?" The mage rested the book in her lap.

"Kemsit and de Cliffe." Hannah let the warm atmosphere of the tower seep into her bones. How could anyone think the light and airy room an evil place? Once they had bookcases made to fit the curved walls, the only place that would rival it for her affections would be the library downstairs. Picking which one she preferred would be like a mother picking a favourite child. Both spaces had a distinct personality that endeared them to her.

"Oh. Truly?" Seraphina pushed the book off her lap to straighten and lower her feet to the floor.

"I was walking in the garden, wondering about Kemsit's influence here, and thought I would try seeing the estate with Anput's eyes. A burst of laughter drew me down an overgrown path, and then I caught glimpses of them. I wouldn't call what I saw true spirits, rather an illusion such as you make when you tell me a story and you create moving pictures." Hannah's fingers itched for a pencil and a sheet of paper. She should draw their faces before they faded from her memory.

Seraphina's fingers curled into the arm of the chaise, and her eyes were bright. "A curious effect that sounds like an echo of something that once happened here. Like a memory being relived."

"Yes! That is what I thought. This was not a ghost reaching out from the Aaru to speak to me, but a glimpse of what once occurred in the garden.

They were in the snow. De Cliffe threw a snowball at Kemsit and she used magic to create a barrage of balls that defeated him." Remembering made a smile play across her lips. The moment had been full of fun and levity.

Her mother laughed. "Your father once made the same mistake. Never throw snowballs at a mischievous mage."

Hannah leaned forward and her hand curled into the fabric of the chaise. "Don't you see, Mother? Enemies do not engage in such activities. It is proof there was a relationship between the two."

"Siblings also play such pranks on each other, as do friends. We cannot leap too far ahead of ourselves." Seraphina pushed off the arm of the chaise and stared out the window. Across the rooftops of Mireworth, the pond was just visible behind the tips of trees.

Hannah stared at the fireplace where the inset panels with their hieroglyphics were clear of all soot. Siblings didn't build each other such towers or sweep them into their arms. "There is more. De Cliffe called himself Kemsit's servant, then he swept her into his arms and carried her off. As she passed me, we locked eyes and she said '*the tower*,' as though it were a clue." That was the piece that confused Hannah. If what she saw was merely an echo from long ago, why had Kemsit repeated those words to her as though she'd seen her?

Seraphina turned back to the rounded room and leaned her hands against the thick window embrasure. "Kemsit was a powerful shadow mage. There are two possibilities. The first was that she knew hundreds of years ago that you would one day stand in that spot, and she planted a clue to help you."

"Which implies she had precognition—knew how events would unfold—and that I would one day seek to unravel the tower's history." That didn't sit right with Hannah. If the mage could foresee the future, why hadn't she done something about Wycliff's ignorant ancestors? Or stopped the death of the infant mage born in Selham centuries later? "What is the second option?"

"That from the Aaru, Kemsit is still somewhat aware of events in the living realm, and she reached across the realms and used the echo as a means to deliver a message to you." Seraphina created a series of spheres in the air. One the green and blue living realm, another the lush yellow and red Duat, and a third, the golden Aaru. They hung in the air like a juggler's balls frozen in mid-throw.

"I think she keeps half an eye on Mireworth and de Cliffe's descendants," Hannah said. When her mother retired to the afterlife, would she also keep a celestial watch over her descendants?

"Which seems more like the action of a maternal figure, rather than a witch intent on cursing this land and family. Not that witches can't be committed to spreading misery among their enemies, but they usually desist once they die. When a soul retreats to the Aaru, it would take incredible effort to reach out through the Duat to touch this realm." The worlds spun and the smaller globe of the Aaru tucked itself back behind the Duat.

"The clue we need is here, Mother." Hannah pointed downward.

Seraphina dropped her gaze to the rug under her feet. "You don't mean this lovely new rug, I suppose, but Kemsit herself."

Hannah met her mother's gaze. "We need to open the sarcophagus," she whispered. A lump formed in her throat, the words dry and tasting of desecration.

"Before we disturb the remains of a powerful shadow mage, perhaps we should finalise Mary and Frank's wedding first?" Seraphina sat on the chaise and patted the spot next to her.

Mary would never forgive Hannah if opening the tomb went horribly wrong and ruined her wedding. It might be prudent to wait a few more days. Besides, gazing upon Kemsit's mummified remains did not seem much like a Christmas Eve type of activity.

5

MARY WOULD BE MARRIED in the pink gown she'd worn to a dance one summer's night. An evening that, in retrospect, seemed a lifetime ago to Hannah. For all that she had worried about the Affliction ending her life, it was the ocean and a selkie that had nearly claimed her, but for the intervention of Wycliff and his childhood friend Lisbeth's soul. Hannah shook off the sad memories and stared at the statue in the centre of the conservatory pool. Once more water flowed from the scales in the brass woman's hands.

Everything in balance, she thought, as the pan on one side filled up and then spilled into the water below. For a moment, the scales levelled out until the water trickled into the pans again.

"Hannah? Is everything all right? You look a

thousand miles away." Her mother reached out and touched her arm.

"Oh. Yes. I was more than a thousand miles away—I was thinking of where to search on our next journey to the Duat." Hannah clutched a paper flower in her fingers. She had been in the process of winding a thin strip of paper around a pencil, making petals with each turn. Once finished, she slid the pencil out and crimped the end underneath to hold it in place.

The bloom went on a pile in the middle of the table. Hannah and her mother took inspiration from Mary's pink dress and the wintry landscape outside as they created the decorations for the conservatory. Mrs Rossett had made a fruitcake and crafted small flowers out of icing to paint and place on top. Today, the women sat in the conservatory's warmth and made garlands of pink and white paper flowers to string around the chairs.

Mary stared at Hannah with wide eyes, a white bloom between her fingers. "It still makes me shudder to hear you talk of visiting the dead, milady. I cannot fathom that they walk and talk just like you and me in some other place...out there." She waved the flower to indicate *out there*.

Seraphina used a magical touch to attach the flowers to a length of ribbon. "It is a difficult concept, Mary. The afterlife is not part of our realm, though it is not dissimilar to the world the

Fae inhabit. The doorways to their worlds are found within our own."

"Well, I for one am quite content with this realm, thank you very much." Mrs Rossett rose from her chair and fetched a tray, then placed the empty teapot and cups on it to take back to the kitchen.

"Only a few days to go now, Mary. Is the excitement keeping you awake at night?" Hannah asked. The new reverend, one who most definitely was not a selkie or any kind of Unnatural creature, would perform the ceremony on Christmas Eve.

Mary sucked on her bottom lip. Then it trembled and her hands fell to her lap, almost crushing the paper flower.

"Whatever is the matter, Mary?" Seraphina set aside the garland. "You would think we were planning your funeral, by the look of you. Are you not excited to marry Frank?"

An all too brief smile flashed across the maid's face. "Oh, yes! But it's what comes afterward..." The bottom lip went from tremble to full-on wobble.

Oh, dear, Hannah thought. It wasn't her place to talk about the marital act with the maid. The very idea made colour rise up her chest. Fortunately, her mother leapt fearlessly into the fray.

"I am sure Frank will be most patient and

gentle on your wedding night, Mary, as he is with the more highly strung horses," Seraphina said.

Mary gasped, and her face turned bright red. "Oh, no! I'm not worried about...*that*. It's that, once I'm married..." Her words trailed off, and she turned watery eyes to Hannah.

"Just blurt it out, Mary, you will feel much better afterward, and then we can help you with whatever it is you are bottling up inside." Hannah wondered what on earth was worrying at the maid.

"You won't want me as your maid anymore," the maid wailed before bursting into tears.

"Whoever told you that?" Hannah had made no such statement, nor did she want to lose the loyal and talented woman. Mary had a gift with styling hair and always knew which gown Hannah wanted to wear.

Mrs Rossett returned from the kitchen with Barnes and a fresh pot of tea. She placed the tray on the table and pulled a handkerchief from her pocket. The hand sat before Mary and offered up the folded cloth that the housekeeper had passed him. Mary took the handkerchief and unfolded it to press to her face and dab at her tears.

"Ladies' maids aren't supposed to be married." The sobs turned into hiccups behind the square of fabric.

Seraphina patted Mary's hand while Mrs

Rossett poured a cup of tea. Barnes fetched a biscuit and placed it on the saucer next to the cup.

It seemed Mary's train of thought had been similar to Hannah's own. "Since when have we followed whatever society does, Mary? I have no intention of letting you go. Unless you no longer wish to work for me?"

Such an idea hadn't occurred to Hannah until now. Would Mary want to devote herself to Frank? What if they had children one day? If such a thing were even possible, given that Frank had died and been assembled from the pieces of several men, before having his heart restarted in an as yet unfathomable process. Hannah blinked firmly to clear her mind before it bolted down that path.

"Oh. No, milady." Mary hiccupped through the words. Then she blew her nose loudly enough to startle the birds roosting on the conservatory roof. "I do want to stay, ever so much."

Relief surged through Hannah. She regarded the maid fondly and didn't want to lose her loyal companionship. Dare she admit it, Hannah was even rather fond of Mary's nerves, and her turns did liven up the day sometimes. "And I do not want to lose you, Mary. We simply have to adjust, that is all. We are all finding our way in this new household."

"Exactly, milady." Mrs Rossett beamed and poured tea for them all. "Much has happened in the last six months and we all have to find our feet. I will say that in my opinion, her ladyship has selected a fine staff for Mireworth and you are all adapting rather well to life here."

"Thank you, Mrs Rossett." It warmed Hannah's insides to hear the housekeeper praise the staff. She had agonised over choosing the right people to fit into their odd household. Laughter often rang out from the servants' hall as they established new friendships and divided up their duties.

The tears subsided once Mary realised she wouldn't face dismissal for marrying the monster she loved. But then her brows pulled together as another worry sprouted in her mind. "Will I have to live apart from Frank, though?" The words quavered and tears threatened anew.

Hannah wished she had an answer to that particular question. It had vexed her for some days. "That is the bit we need to figure out, Mary. I know you will want to be with your husband. But I must say, I don't like the idea of your living out in the stables with the horses."

An enormous sigh heaved through the maid. "Neither do I, milady. I do so long to have a place we could call our own, with a little parlour where we could sit at night."

"What about the cottage in the garden?" Mrs Rossett suggested.

"What cottage in the garden?" Hannah hadn't

noticed one in her explorations, although parts of the estate were so overgrown it wouldn't surprise her to discover an entire castle concealed in the neglected undergrowth.

"It's tucked in beside the kitchen garden. It used to be for the head gardener, and it's not too far from either the house or the stables." The house-keeper took a sip of her tea and Barnes rushed to fetch her a biscuit.

"Let us see." Seraphina conjured a map of the estate that hovered above the teapot. She touched the walled kitchen garden that provided their produce, and that area grew larger. Then, with a fingertip, she rotated the map so they could see on the other side of the wall.

"That's it. There." Mrs Rossett pointed to a large brooding mass that flowed over the wall and draped across the grass, rather like a waterfall of brambles.

"Are you sure?" Hannah squinted. It did have a rough squarish shape. When she peered closer, a chimney jutted up like a hand waving for help in the ocean. Vines clambered over its side, and bushes across the front obscured it from view as though the plants concealed Sleeping Beauty's tower.

"Oh. No wonder I don't recollect it. The garden has claimed it as its own." Hannah's hand hovered above the image. Mireworth concealed much beneath her surface.

"It looks like a frightful amount of work, milady." Mary leaned forward to frown at the stone structure.

"I don't think it will take too much at all, Mary. I think a few days of hard work and a touch of magic would clear this away." Seraphina stroked the vine, and it crumbled away from the stone. Next she trimmed the bushes to small rounded shapes. Others were removed entirely by smudging a fingertip over them. A few more flicks of the mage's hand, and the stone and windows were scrubbed. Bright pink geraniums and dahlias sprouted around the door of the cottage, and smoke curled from the chimney.

"Oh! It's lovely." Mary let out a sigh and clasped her hands to her chest.

Hannah agreed with the maid. The spruced-up cottage would have a charming and welcoming appearance. If only the actual work could be accomplished as easily as the mage altered the image floating above the table. "That is settled, then. We will clear away the overgrown plants from the cottage, see to any repairs, and make it a welcoming home for Mary and Frank."

"It will be a lovely home, and Mary will still be close enough to assist you at night when you require it, Hannah. I can ensorcel a bell to enable you to ring for Mary if she is not inside Mireworth," Seraphina said.

"Thank you both. You are ever so kind to me." Mary burst into tears again, but at least this time they were tears of happiness.

IN THEIR CAREFUL budgeting of where to spend their recently acquired wealth, Hannah demanded that one job be undertaken as a matter of priority— restoring the library to its original proportions. Fortunately, it wasn't as difficult as they thought to knock down the hastily erected wall that had sliced the room in half. The workmen Wycliff's grandfather employed hadn't done a very good job. Hannah enjoyed watching the wall to the billiards room tumble into dust under the sledgehammer wielded by Frank.

The men built a new wall in the original location, and once again the library had two soaring windows and an enormous fireplace. The gantry and spiral staircase now clung to a blank wall. The labour-intensive cabinetwork to create new bookshelves would take longer, but Hannah could wait, knowing the job would be worth it when three walls of shelves cried out for books to fill their empty expanses.

Before they had both departed London for

their country homes, Hannah and Lizzie had spent many an hour discussing appropriate colours for the library. The one in the duke's Mayfair home was resplendent in red and gold, but Hannah had used Percy the peacock as her inspiration. Rugs in hues of soft green and mossy khaki were found to scatter across the floor. A chaise in rich blue velvet sat before the fire, with a brown leather armchair on either side. The arrangement reminded Hannah of the way the plain peahens sat on either side of the peacock.

Drapes in blue and green striped silk tumbled from the high ceiling and down either side of the windows. A brocade that replicated the eye on a feather covered the squabs of the window seats and smaller cushions on the chaise. The chandelier, with its muted brass arms, cast a soft light over those below, like the way the sunlight filtered through the trees in a glade.

Hannah delighted in curling up in the restored space. Today, she sat with a journal open on her lap. She penned her own story about Mireworth and the secrets she uncovered, the work they undertook, and her dreams for the future. Here she had also sketched portraits of Kemsit and de Cliffe from memory.

Her mother sat at the large desk, the original plans for the gardens spread out before her. Tiny trees and waterways flowed over the paper as the mage considered what to restore first and what plantings would be altered in the new fashion. While Hannah appreciated a beautiful garden, she much preferred to run through hedges than trim them. She was content to leave final decisions in her mother's capable hands.

An urgent call had summoned her father and Timmy away, as a man had fallen from his horse and badly broken his leg. The surgeon's skill had been requested to save the limb. As the family settled into the community, even the prickly apothecary, Mr Seager, became civil when they met. Sir Hugh consulted with him when he treated the villagers, and the two men had taken to walking out across the meadows when the weather allowed, discussing ailments and their cures.

Before the fire, Wycliff stretched out on the chaise with a book in his hands. But every time Hannah glanced up, he appeared to be studying her and not the page. Barnes continued to examine every inch of Mireworth he could reach, inspired by their discovery in the Tudor dining room. Hannah found the hand an invaluable accomplice in the search, and they had crossed two more rooms off the map after they yielded nothing.

That evening, Barnes paced up and down the empty bookshelves, rapping with the pads of his fingers every step. At times, he retraced his steps, knocked again, scuttled forward and knocked before repeating the process. A quick succession of snaps caught Hannah's attention, and she set down the book and pen. Barnes waved from a point halfway along the shelves.

"What is it, Barnes?" She swung her feet to the floor.

The hand waggled one finger and pointed to a spot underneath him.

"Found something?" Wycliff asked as he rose and joined her.

"Let us hope it is another musty old journal. Now Barnes has the scent of it, he might sniff them out like a truffle pig." Seraphina altered the map before her, replacing a walk of birches with espaliered copper beech.

Hannah knelt on the floor before the hand, and Wycliff crouched beside her. When Barnes had their attention, he rapped on the spot below him. Then he paced to the next shelf and tapped, before rushing back to the first spot and banging again.

"You're right, it does sound different." Wycliff ran his hands over the shelf. "There's no seam or crack, though."

"A hidden catch, perhaps?" Seraphina suggested from the desk, where a diminutive grotto now sprouted.

Wycliff examined all the joins of the shelving. Man and hand pushed on every knot or depression, hoping to find a hidden lever. Hannah did the same on the other side. Minutes passed, but they found nothing that triggered any secret compartment.

"If there is a latch, it is located somewhere other than here," Wycliff said. Not to be defeated, he returned to the desk and plucked a letter opener from its spot holding down a corner of the map. "I think his lordship is allowed to take a knife to the library," he muttered.

Kneeling beside Hannah, he eased the sharp blade between the skirting and shelf. Inch by inch, Wycliff levered the nails free until a twelve inch run of skirting pulled loose and revealed a shadowy space under the shelf.

Barnes leapt to the floor and disappeared into the narrow gap. From within came intriguing rustles and scrapes, before the hand emerged dragging a book.

"Oh! Well done, Barnes, another one. You really can detect them." Hannah patted the hand.

Wycliff picked up the old journal and shook it free of dust. Hannah leaned against his side as he opened the cover and read the date at the top of the page. "Sixteen ninety-nine. Over a hundred years after the last journal Barnes found and just two years before Mireworth was built."

Seraphina chuckled. "You were right, Hannah. Wycliff's ancestors did indeed secrete accounts around the house. Let us hope this one sheds some light on our many questions."

Wycliff flicked open the old journal and angled it toward the light cast from the chandelier to better read the spidery script aloud.

"'I no longer believe the old tales that de Cliffe traded his life for that of his heir. If it were true, that one of us was to be given the devil as a minion of Hell, why has Lucifer never collected on the deal? And yet...the tower remains. The witch cursed this family with the blasted ugly thing, and no more will I tolerate her presence. But my men have laboured for a week with hammers and pick-axes and not a single chip has been dislodged from that monstrosity.'"

"He tried to tear down the tower!" Hannah exclaimed. And how ironic that she and Wycliff planned to tear down part of Mireworth to expose the tower to sunlight once more.

6

SERAPHINA GESTURED in the direction of the tower beyond the library. "The binding spell in the fireplace keeps every stone in place. Neither man nor nature will shake so much as a pebble loose. Luckily, the Wycliff of old never peered into the fireplace. Not that he would have known about the spell, unless he could read hieroglyphics and he had the co-operation of a mage powerful enough to undo Kemsit's work."

"Why did the tower allow *you* to create a doorway in the stone, Mother?" Hannah asked.

The mage waved her hands, and the trees on the map before her sank back into the paper. "Because a shadow mage cast the binding spell, and a shadow mage asked the tower to admit us. The spell is an unusual one, imbued with the power of Duat. The tower will endure until a shadow mage releases it to sink into the ground."

An enduring symbol that would stand throughout time—but a symbol of what? Pieces of a mosaic fell into place in Hannah's mind. She refused to believe that anything evil or with malicious intent would be gifted with such longevity by the Duat or by Anubis. For centuries, Wycliff's ancestors had been wrong about both the tower and Kemsit. How delicious that a shadow mage and her daughter would reveal the truth.

"If there is ever an earthquake, we should seek shelter in the tower, then," Wycliff said. "Not sure if its durability would be much use against an invading army, though."

"I'm sure that between the two of us, we could add a moat of lava." Seraphina laughed.

Hannah nudged Wycliff with an elbow. "We don't need defensive fortifications. Keep reading, please."

Wycliff cleared his throat and used a fingertip to find his place on the page.

"'Since it cannot be destroyed, let it be forgotten. Plans will be drawn to smother the stain and wipe it from our lives. I have written to the mage council and they have agreed to cast a spell over Selham, to obfuscate any memory of the witch and the tower from the minds of the locals.'"

"That is a clear violation of the mage council's

directive." Seraphina pushed back from the desk to pace before the wall of shelves. "To alter people's memories is a dangerous path and something one mage alone cannot do. They must have known the rumours of Kemsit's time here, and sought to erase her from history."

"That would also explain why no one around here could shed any light on the history of the tower. Except for Mr Hartley." Not that the selkie had much of use to share.

"Unnaturals do not respond in the same way to magic as ordinary humans do. It is possible that he and his grandmother did not feel the effects of any such spell to conceal both tower and Kemsit." The mage stalked to the fireplace and gripped the mantel with one hand.

Hannah grinned at her mother. "After all that time and effort, they have failed. For we will bring her back into the light, now that a shadow mage sits on the council."

Seraphina turned and winked at her daughter, her mood lightening. "Serves them right for trying to keep we troublesome women under their thumb."

"I do feel I should speak up in defence of my sex. Not all men are idiots." Wycliff arched an eyebrow at Hannah.

She kissed his cheek. "Quite right. Some are enlightened and noble of spirit."

"And strong enough to walk alongside a troublesome woman." Seraphina raised a phantom glass to toast Wycliff.

He bowed his head to her in return. Then he continued to flick through the pages of the journal. "Here, this is interesting... 'The witch's influence remains. The tiles in the entrance hall are no longer the geometric design that is fashionable. Day by day, they have turned a dirty brown, as though a horde of children has run across them with muddy feet. Now, heathen creatures appear from the murk and a ridiculous river flows from her tower. She is a rot, seeping from that damned building.'"

"I am glad I did not meet your great-grandfather, Wycliff. I do not think I would have liked him. He seems most determined to cast Kemsit in some evil role because she changed the tiles." Hannah considered the tiled landscape one of her favourite features of the house. Even on a cold and grey winter's day, she could stroll the lush growth on the banks of the Nile and remember the dry heat of the Duat. That led her to wonder how the shadow mage could have achieved such a thing so long after her death. Had the mage been so powerful that even after she retired to the Aaru, her very remains influenced things around her? "How do you think she did that, Mother?"

Her mother tapped her long fingers on the cool marble mantel. "It is possible that the spot held great meaning for her, and so an impression of her vibrates up from the ground and through whatever is laid atop it. For all we know, it might once have been the spot where she had her chamber, or a garden. Much like the glade at our Westbourne Green home means the world to me. If someone tiled over it, I might vex the new owner by having an image of Percy in full display appear in the new surface."

Wycliff passed the journal to Hannah. "There is more about the history of the tower and house here, but I do not think it will answer your questions about de Cliffe and Kemsit."

She clutched the journal to her. The more she found, the less she trusted the words left by Wycliff's ancestors. Having seen the echo of the couple in the garden, the truth now resonated through her. They had been happy, and Kemsit was no more evil than her mother. "I don't think any account written long after they left this earth will answer our questions. What we need is an account in de Cliffe's own hand, or Kemsit's."

"If there ever was such a record, I can't see it being hidden in Mireworth. The house is little more than a hundred years old." He rubbed a hand over the back of his neck and his brows knitted together as he considered other options. "Anything that might have once been stored in the old castle would have been lost centuries ago when it was pulled down."

"Which leaves only the possibility of an account hidden somewhere that has *endured* through the years," Seraphina mused.

Hannah nearly smacked herself in the forehead at the obvious answer. "The tower and Kemsit's sarcophagus. Those are the only things that have stood here undisturbed. I do not think I can wait until after Mary's wedding to open it."

A shaft of sunlight burst through the clouds outside and a bright finger reached into the room.

Seraphina gestured to the sunny patch and passed a hand through it. "Ah! A change in the weather. Almost as though Kemsit is asking that we leave her undisturbed for another day. This is just the opportunity to send the men out on another task, Hannah, before the rain returns."

"Of course. Let us seize the break in the weather." Hannah tucked a bemused smile inside herself. Her mother had expressed an odd idea involving a tree, and needed the men to go out and find the perfect specimen.

"I shall fetch Frank and your father for this undertaking, but there is one thing before I depart." Wycliff pulled a small piece of greenery from his pocket and dangled it over Hannah's head.

"Wherever did you find that?" She glanced up

at the mistletoe and then placed a chaste kiss on his lips. Her mother was watching, after all.

He grinned. "Frank has taken to carrying a sprig in his pocket and stealing kisses from Mary. I thought it a brilliant idea, and found my own."

Hannah picked up Barnes, who no doubt would want to assist the men. Then they left the library to find the others. In the rear vestibule that faced the courtyard and stables, the men bundled up in warm coats and hats. They ventured out with axes and a saw in the back of the cart, Barnes in his customary position on Frank's shoulder. Hannah giggled at the sight. They looked like a desperate hunting party searching for food in a desolate arctic wilderness.

"It is difficult to believe the fearsome prey they stalk is a tree," Hannah murmured, her words frosting on the air.

"A rather large tree, I hope. It is a German tradition, and one I thought you might like to try," Seraphina said as they waved off the hunters. She linked her arm through Hannah's. "Shall we prepare for their return? I would like to discuss its placement with you."

The large drawing room, where during his first visit to Mireworth Hannah's father had built a fort under a table, was turned into a Christmas wonderland. Since this was Hannah's first holiday season at Mireworth and also the first for their new staff, she had spent long nights agonising over how to make it a special event. She also wanted to establish traditions that they would all look forward to in the years to come.

First the two women decided on a corner to one side of the fireplace for the tree, should the men prove successful in their expedition.

"We could add boughs of greenery and twist them with holly along the mantel?" Hannah suggested.

"Most definitely. A tiny ensorcelled mushroom in each will cast a pretty light similar to a candle. Then I can add a touch of magical snow to them." Seraphina threw her hands in the air and a shower of fat snowflakes fell from the ceiling.

With the assistance of Mary and Hollie, the new maid, the women set off on their own foray into the grounds, each carrying a basket. They trimmed greenery from the hedges and then snipped bits of holly with bright red berries from a hedgerow. The piles of cuttings were heaped on the rug in the middle of the drawing room floor. Hannah spent a pleasant afternoon with her mother, crafting the pieces into decorations and placing them around the room.

They were clearing away the remains of stems and leaves when a loud banging heralded the return of the men.

Wycliff's clear voice called, "This way!"

That was followed by a few curses and a dramatic *Ouch!* The drawing-room door banged open and the tip of a large tree poked through. Hannah and Seraphina moved to one side as it drifted into the room like a large green ship attempting to moor in harbour.

Hannah hardly dared look as the men manoeuvred the tree into position. When they stepped back to admire their handiwork, she let out a soft gasp. Even unadorned, the spruce made an imposing sight. At twelve feet tall, it didn't quite reach the high ceiling. Frank stood beside it and held the tree upright and, for once, was dwarfed by his companion.

"Once we make it secure, we can decorate it." Excitement sparkled in Seraphina's eyes.

"Decorate a tree?" Hannah wondered if her mother had remembered the German tradition correctly.

"Yes. Candles are often placed on the boughs, along with brightly coloured garlands." Seraphina waved her hands around the tree.

"Lighted candles nestled among the spruce? And you think my hellhound form is a fire hazard," Wycliff huffed.

"How do we keep it alive and upright? Poor Frank cannot stand there for the next two weeks," Hannah said.

"I shall take care of that." The shadow mage

knelt on the ground before the tree and placed her hands palm down before it. Words of magic whispered around the room and a faint breeze stirred the tree's boughs. A creak and groan echoed along the floorboards and the tree dropped an inch in height, as though the floor had given way beneath it. When Seraphina sat back on her heels, a mossy mound sprouted around the base of the tree as though it had always grown in that spot and the house had been constructed around it. The faint aroma of fresh leaves filtered into the room.

Hannah thought it marvellous to have a small piece of the forest in the drawing room. Perhaps they could create paper owls to peer out from the branches.

Wycliff slid his arms around her waist and pulled her closer to his chest. "This is shaping up to be the most incredible Christmas the old house has ever seen."

She shared his sentiment. As each day passed, it seemed a little more magic spread through Mireworth. Her heart warmed to think of the years to come under its roof.

"To avoid setting fire to the house, I have another idea instead of lighted candles for the tree." Seraphina studied the spruce. Then she whispered in a singsong and fluttered her fingers through the air as though she mimicked a butterfly's wings.

Dozens of fireflies appeared, and buzzed

around the mage. They spiralled around her, then she stroked her hand sideways and they followed the motion. The flickering lights flowed toward the tree. Some went high, some low, and others burrowed between the branches. Seraphina changed their placement, plucking a firefly from one area and setting it in another. Several minutes passed before she was satisfied with her work and the spruce wore a sparkling gown of tiny yellow winking lights.

"Should we place something on the very top of the tree?" Hannah stared at the apex. In shape, it somewhat resembled a pyramid from Egypt. "Something golden, to remind us of the Duat and those who are not with us this winter."

"Let me think..." Seraphina tilted her head and then took a step backward. She brought her hands toward her chest, whispered to her closed palms, and then broke them upward as though she released a dove.

A glint caught Hannah's eye as something streaked toward the tree. The yellow blur formed itself into the eye of Horus in gleaming gold atop the tree. "To watch over us. Or perhaps Kemsit will peer out from it, to see how she is remembered," Seraphina said.

The idea caught fire in Hannah's imagination. If Kemsit were indeed watching over the family, why couldn't they have a ritual that thanked her and recognised the part she played in their lives?

More ideas radiated out from that one. What little they'd found that mentioned either the tower or Kemsit had been written by Wycliff's male ancestors. Where were the women's voices? How she longed to learn what a succession of Lady Wycliffs thought of their unusual resident.

"What do you say to a little indoor snow, Hannah?" Her mother's cheerful voice brought her mind back to the current task.

"Oh, yes. On the tips of the branches, please," Hannah said.

With another sliding gesture, Seraphina added a light dusting of snow to the tree. Then, as though she had read Hannah's mind, she dabbed a finger at one spot near the back of the tree.

Movement caught Hannah's eye, then it disappeared. Two yellow eyes did a slow blink. A small owl with cream and buff feathers nestled on a branch.

Hannah let out a sigh. Perfect. They should have a tree every Christmas. Who knew, they might start a new fashion.

7

AFTER DINNER, and despite their previous resolutions to wait, Hannah and her mother visited Kemsit's tomb. The mage had installed glow lamps around the edge of the tower room and they emitted a soft pink light reminiscent of the exterior stonework. Seraphina rested her palms on the sarcophagus and murmured a greeting under her breath to the deceased shadow mage.

"Tell me again what Anubis told you of Kemsit and de Cliffe," Hannah asked. When they had journeyed to Duat, the god of the underworld had promised to reveal the tale if Seraphina took the position of shadow mage at his side. She, in turn, had related the few details when they returned to Westbourne Green.

"Anubis may be a god of the underworld, but

he is no storyteller. We have only the bare bones of the story, with no embellishments or flavour of character to satisfy you." Seraphina huffed a soft laugh.

Hannah touched Kemsit's tomb. "Oh, do tell me again, Mother, please. There may yet be a clue in the tale that we can puzzle out."

"Very well. As you know, de Cliffe answered the call to crusade in the Holy Land. War did not go well for him, and he suffered a mortal wound. He crawled into a temple where Kemsit was defending the acolytes from the Crusaders. He begged Kemsit to heal him, promising her anything in return. For some reason that Anubis skims over, Kemsit agreed to try and save him. While restoring his life was beyond her power, she told de Cliffe that she knew someone who could. She summoned Anubis, who struck the bargain with Wycliff's ancestor. A hellhound had somehow been slaughtered in the fighting, which rather annoyed Anubis. If de Cliffe promised his heir as a replacement hound, he would restore the soldier to health."

"'One of mine for one of yours, a bargain struck, the tower endures,'" Hannah whispered the words carved into a stone laid in the floor.

Seraphina created pink lotus blossoms from the air and laid them around the tomb. "After that campaign in Egypt ended, Kemsit journeyed to

England with de Cliffe to ensure he kept his end of the bargain. Or so Anubis claims."

They had added two softly padded chairs to the tomb, and they took their seats quietly before it. Hannah stared at the sarcophagus as she gathered her thoughts. Being in the silent and comforting tomb was rather like sitting in a quiet church and seeking wisdom.

"Yet if we start to pick at the story, it unravels. Anubis did not take de Cliffe's heir. There was a span of many generations before Wycliff was bitten by the hellhound. There are so many questions that do not fit the narrative. Why would Kemsit summon Anubis to heal an invader? If she were defending the temple against the Crusaders, she should have ended him. Nor did the bargain struck require her to travel to England to live with him. Most perplexing of all, I cannot understand why de Cliffe built this tower to house her sarcophagus."

What journals they had found by Wycliff's ancestors showed a distinct dislike, bordering on hatred, for Kemsit and her tower. Hannah stared upward at the stone ceiling. When she picked at the words left by Wycliff's ancestors, they didn't fit into the spaces of the puzzle she completed in her mind. Hatred and dislike were the wrong shape and size. Whispers swirling around her suggested that she needed a piece containing family and love.

"None of this strikes me as the actions of two people who are enemies."

"Ah. We are of one mind on that. Hate does not explain how events unfolded. But I suspect love does." Seraphina's eyes sparkled like sapphires in the low light.

Hannah recalled everything she knew and cast it in a different light—that of a romantic fairy tale rather than a horror story. "Kemsit and de Cliffe simply had to have known each other before that day he crawled into the temple. The Crusaders were in Egypt for years and I suspect their paths crossed before that particular battle. What if he made his way to that temple because he knew she was inside? Kemsit did whatever she could to save his life because she loved him."

She paused at that point in the tale. Memories flooded over her. Wycliff and her mother had both challenged Anubis and demanded that the god of the underworld restore Hannah to life. Only in the face of their love had the jackal-headed god complied and allowed his wife, Anput, to restart Hannah's heart.

"I choose to believe that Kemsit left her home in Egypt to come to a cold and grey England to be with him, not because Anubis compelled her to." Hannah could imagine the shock to the shadow mage when she stepped off the ship—the golden sand and dry heat of the desert replaced by dreary rain and green meadows.

Seraphina gestured to the tower. "This tower is itself a tribute to love, not the imprisonment of an enemy. From the pale pink stone to the careful construction, it is shaped as a circle, which is never-ending, like true love."

Hannah blew out a sigh. Before her lay the secret of Mireworth. A shadow mage whose existence had been carefully erased from the mage council records, and then hidden by Wycliff's family. They had proof in the journal that the council had set an enchantment over the village to make the people of Selham forget both shadow mage and tower. And then they had enclosed it, permanently out of sight.

Her body itched to fill in the missing pieces. The more they found that pointed in the wrong direction, the more convinced she became that Mireworth concealed a great love story, not a tragedy or a horror.

"If we hold to our version as being the true account, we still don't know why Wycliff's ancestors regarded the tower with such...shame. Do you think it was the fact she was a shadow mage that they objected to, or that she was a woman?" Hannah paced to the corner where the stone with the inscription lay. *One of mine for one of yours, a bargain struck, the tower endures.*

Her mother snorted. "Knowing how men react to things, the fact she was a woman would have bothered them most. If a male shadow mage had walked this land, I am convinced the mage council would have crowned him their leader. Until men and women like that are forced to confront their fears, they will never change." Sparks rose from Seraphina as her temper flared and a thousand fire-flies spun around the room.

Hannah reached out and caught a dancing spark that reminded her of the piece of soul impris-oned in glass shards by Dupré. "Hypothesise, then strategize. The echo I witnessed in the grounds was of a happy couple. You do not laugh and play with an enemy in such a way, and there was joy in Kemsit's eyes when she looked at me. We have the bones of a story that feels right. We must now find the details to flesh out the true version, so we can record the correct history. I am convinced that *somewhere* we will find a hidden account."

Seraphina waved her arms, and the fireflies joined up and became a string of tiny lights draped from the ceiling, as though they sat in a fairy grotto. "Armed with the year de Cliffe most likely returned to England from Egypt, I searched the mage records again. After days shut in their dreary library combing through old tomes, I found a single paragraph that refers to Kemsit. Long ago, a mage recorded that a dead Egyptian witch had reached our shores and that her presence would not be tolerated."

"Do you think they...ended her?" Hannah's eyes widened as she imagined a mob waving torches. How sad that some events repeated themselves; two Afflicted had been erased in a similar fiery fashion. Those who continued to exist after their hearts had stopped caused an illogical fear in some people.

"I have considered that possibility, but I do not think so. If she were burned, I doubt her remains would emit the faint magical mist that permeates the tower. I believe she is intact within, and whatever the council planned, she outwitted them." Seraphina created the illusion of a pond, where she set lotus blooms to float upon the aqua water. An iridescent dragonfly darted from one flower to another.

A chuckle welled up in Hannah's chest. From the stories her mother told, the mage council did not take it well when bested by a woman. "In a span of six hundred years, two women had the advantage over them. No wonder the mage council is so bitter—their egos have not yet recovered."

Her mother barked in laughter, her humour unrestrained. "Three women, my dear one. Do not forget that not long after Kemsit came here, a mage spirited away a baby girl and she grew into a woman who not only defied the council, but our very nature, by having three gifted girls by her Unnatural lover."

"Of course, the legend of the Crows." How could Hannah have forgotten her favourite bedtime tale? In her mind, she added Kemsit's advising the old mage how to shelter the babe until she came of age.

Her mother added a pile of rocks to one side of the pond and water trickled over them. "While it is not worthy of us to mock the council, they do let pride get the better of them. There was hundreds of years of hot air stuffed inside that council room when I finally broke through and let a fresh breeze within."

"This adds to our story. Whatever action the mage council planned to take, it failed. Kemsit's physical remains are still here at Mireworth. I wonder about the snippet Wycliff found in his great-grandfather's journal, where he wrote that the council cast a spell over this region. Is it possible they did something similar to this family, that the men carry such ill feelings about the tower?" Hannah stared at the sarcophagus, wondering how far the influence of the mage council extended in Selham. Her mother said that while mages could not pluck memories directly from the minds of the villagers, they could attach confusion to a person or object that would veil them in a thick mist.

"That is possible. But it was so long ago I suspect any such spell has eroded over time. Wycliff seemed indifferent to the tower and knew nothing of its resident. I dare say if there were any residual spell, it rubbed off once he began associating with us." Satisfied with the peaceful decorations added to Kemsit's tomb, her mother took the seat next to Hannah.

"You did say I would smooth his rough edges. You forgot to add 'and remove any lingering effects of a long-ago spell.'" While her husband still barely clung to the most basic of manners in company, he had an open mind and was capable of change or admitting when he was wrong. For her part, Hannah had stepped into a role as a voice for those who needed one. No longer did she mutter from the shadows about the injustices of the world.

She also admitted to it on those rare occasions when she was wrong. Wycliff made a great show of writing such instances in the little notebook he carried in his coat pocket.

"We are still left with the mystery of what happened and whether the mage council ventured here. De Cliffe built the tower while Kemsit still *lived* here and it is fair to assume the room above was her private solar, such as your turret at Westbourne Greene." Had the couple planned for the day Kemsit would retire from this realm to the world of the Duat? Hannah glanced sideways at her mother. Did her parents discuss what would happen when her father's mortal span was ended?

Shaking aside such a sad eventuality, Hannah considered the tomb. Kemsit must have instructed the stonemason who built her sarcophagus, as no one else would have known the hieroglyphics to inscribe. Nor could one man alone move the heavy slab that formed the lid.

"You want to open it now, don't you?" her mother spoke in a soft tone from beside her.

"Yes and no." Hannah rose from her chair and stood beside the tomb. One hand hovered over the granite. "If you slumbered here, I would be upset if anyone broke open your tomb to gawk at your remains and satisfy their curiosity. Part of me still wishes to disturb her sleep, even though I know it is a slim hope that she might be clutching a scroll that will answer all my questions."

Seraphina chuckled and joined Hannah. She brushed a hand over one of the plain sides of the sarcophagus. "All this space where she could have carved the entire story for us. I wonder why she did not tell her story, as is common in Egyptian tombs."

"Oh!" Hannah knelt on the ground, excitement building inside her. She ran her hands over the smooth and unadorned stone. "What if she did?"

Her mother cocked her head. "You think the story is here, but she used the carving equivalent of invisible ink?" Seraphina gracefully lowered herself to the ground to sit beside her daughter. She caressed the granite with long fingers and murmured in a low tone. Beneath her fingertips, a flash of hieroglyphics appeared before sinking back into the stone. "Look, Hannah! You are right. There is indeed a spell embedded in the granite."

Then an idea plunged through Hannah with cold disappointment. "What if it has worn off, like the spell the mage council cast, and we cannot retrieve what was once written?"

Seraphina scoffed. "The council tried to meddle in people's memories. That sort of interference never sticks. Mother Nature would have quietly brushed it away like waves lapping at rock. Leaving a story only certain people can read is a different matter entirely. And let us not forget about her binding spell in the fireplace. It would apply equally to any spell cast over her tomb."

Hope surged again inside Hannah, along with a vague sense of nausea, as her stomach protested the extreme range of emotions. "Can you reveal what is hidden here?"

"With a little time, yes. All I need is the correct incantation to trigger the story into revealing itself. Then it will take some time to translate, I suspect." Her mother patted the stone as she rose from the cool floor.

Hannah sighed. More waiting. Very well. At least she carried the excitement of discovering that

Kemsit had recorded her story, but kept it private from certain critical eyes. "Turning to another matter. Do you think she should be moved somewhere more...appropriate?"

"You mean like a churchyard? Her beliefs are not ours. I cannot think of anywhere more appropriate than here. She is an integral part of Mireworth."

Hannah thought so, too, but having a long-dead mage under their roof wasn't for everyone. "I feel we should do something to show our respect and yet celebrate how she moulded Wycliff's family."

Seraphina walked to the doorway she had created by removing select stones. "What if we created an ironwork door here, one that allows a glimpse inside her tomb, but keeps out those who are overly curious or intent on damage?"

"Yes, I like that idea. Perhaps a gate with the hieroglyphics of her name on it?" Hannah already had plans to add a padded bench under the window in the adjoining room, so she could either gaze outside at the driveway or inside at the tower.

"I can ask the tower to allow us to trim up the stonework to fit a gate." Seraphina constructed the illusion of one that shimmered and preserved her fellow shadow mage's privacy.

"She will be brought into the light," Hannah murmured. How would she hold her patience, waiting for her mother to determine if the story they sought had been right before them all this time? Then her stomach gurgled and Hannah placed a hand over it. All this excitement really didn't agree with her.

"Excuse me, Mother." On quick feet, she rushed to find an open window or an empty pot before her stomach rebelled.

8

An ODD MALAISE swept over Hannah for the next few days, so she set aside planned explorations and forays about the house and estate. Instead, she devoted her time to her journals and particularly the one detailing life with Barnes. Perhaps one day in the future, tales of the disembodied hand would amuse readers. It also gave him a small measure of immortality, to compensate for the loss of his body.

Today, she had a green woollen blanket wrapped around her as she lay on the chaise in the tower room. Snow flurries blew past the window, but there wasn't enough substance to it to settle on the ground. While the temperature in the tower fell, and despite the bite of cold battering the windows, the solar remained one of her favourite spots. She loved gazing out over the rooftops to the grounds beyond. The wind whipped the tree branches and birds hurried to find protection from the weather.

Soon Hannah would have to relocate to the library, as even the blanket failed to keep her toes warm. Nor could the rugs scattered over the floor raise the ambient temperature. Each space they restored had its own appeal, but there was a particular reason she sought the refuge of the tower—the solitude. While they only used a dozen rooms in the enormous and rambling house, Hannah hadn't shared a home with so many people since her parents had gone off to war and left her in the care of Lady Loburn.

Her parents kept only a few staff at Westbourne Green, and Hannah needed time to become accustomed to sharing her life with all the new faces. Footmen and maids went about their day, nodding or offering shy smiles as Hannah passed them in the halls. Voices rang out from the kitchen and servants' quarters. With each person who joined the household, Mireworth drew a deeper breath into her lungs and roused into life. In an odd way, Hannah mourned the loss of the days of using Wycliff's study as a bedroom and when everyone spent time in the warm kitchen.

A chill swept down her spine, and Hannah pulled her blanket closer around her shoulders. They had tried lighting the fire in the solar, but smoke billowed back into the room. Only now had she decided to investigate the blockage. She had requested Barnes' assistance when Mrs Rossett could spare him. The two had become quite inseparable and the hand often helped with the baking and preparation of meals. A scuffling from the stone stairs heralded his arrival, and Hannah set aside the journal and her blanket as Barnes scuttled across the floor.

"Barnes, I have quite the task for you." They contemplated the towering fireplace looming over the hand. Hannah peered up into the enormous chimney, but couldn't see anything obvious.

A few days before, Wycliff had reached up with his extra height, but had not felt any obstruction. Timmy offered to scamper up, but Hannah baulked at the idea of sending the lad up so high. At least Barnes was an adult, despite his short stature.

"Are you sure you will be all right up there?" she asked Barnes.

The hand would crawl up the brickwork to pull free what she assumed would be decades of birds' nests wedged in the space. He gave a thumbs up. Hannah tied a length of twine to his wrist in case he became stuck and she had to haul him out. She stood inside the fireplace and lifted him up as far as she could reach. The chimney had an irregular surface, and using his fingertips, he swung from outcrop to outcrop as he climbed upward.

Time ticked by, accompanied by a scrabbling and chunks of ash falling back into the fireplace. Hannah stepped clear, lest she be covered in soot, as Barnes continued his exploration. The noise changed in pitch and frequency. Then came a slow scrape, followed by a thud as a large object landed in the hearth.

Hannah gasped, thinking Barnes had fallen. Then, on assessing the shape and size of the lump lying still in the dust, she realised she was mistaken.

"What have you found?" Hannah murmured as she peered at the item.

Stirred-up soot created a black snowstorm. Specks swirled within the space and she had to wait for them to settle or risk staining her skin and clothes with the inky mist. Then she dragged the item closer. Whatever it was, it appeared to be wrapped in oilskin cloth and tied with string.

Barnes swung down and pointed to the item and then up into the chimney.

"I gather this is what was blocking the chimney?" Hannah untied the twine from the hand's wrist stump.

Yes, he signalled.

"Let us see what someone hid up there." Hannah pulled her folding knife from her pocket and sliced the twine. Then she unwrapped the parcel. A gasp caught in her throat as the freed prisoner revealed itself. Refracted light danced around the room, and the contents sparkled—far more beautiful than any quick charcoal drawing could capture. Tucked next to the item, she found two notes. One had been addressed to Lady Wycliff, the other to Jonas.

There were two possibilities. One, that whoever hid the parcel had done so within recent memory and the note was intended for the Jonas Hannah had married. The other scenario was that the parcel had been concealed for decades and some other man named Jonas was the intended recipient. Yet...given what Barnes had discovered, Hannah believed Wycliff's mother had been responsible for their find.

Putting aside the sealed note for her husband, Hannah picked up the one for Lady Wycliff. Hannah glanced around the room. Not seeing any shades or lost souls of the previous women to bear that title, she decided to read the note on their behalf. She carried the bundle to one of the over-sized floor cushions and curled up on the velvety softness. Placing the gems in her lap, she slid a nail under the seal and unfolded the sheet of paper.

She scanned a few lines, and a gasp caught in her throat. Then Barnes tapped at her knee. Of course. How rude to keep him in suspense when it was his discovery. Starting from the top, she read aloud.

To the Lady Wycliff who finds this,

If you are married to my Jonas, I hope that you find much joy in your union. While an intense and oftentimes argumentative child, he is fiercely loyal and loving. I have no doubt he will prove to be the best husband to the woman who holds his heart. Please treat it with kindness.

If you are reading this after finding my parcel in the tower chimney, know that this room has offered a retreat to countless Lady Wycliffs; I am only sorry I could not show you to this hidden place, nor could it be a place of shared confidences. I do not know what, if anything, you know about this family's history. My husband and I argued about many things, but on one topic we were in agreement. Jonas was not told the old tale. For my husband, that was to protect him from the curse. I rather think it saved him from inheriting hundreds of years of prejudice.

Hannah snorted at the last sentence. Wycliff knew of the tower's existence from having found it as a boy, but had indeed been saved from the incorrect version of events passed from father to son.

Family legend has it that many years ago, after he lost his wife giving birth to his son and heir, de Cliffe answered the call to the Crusades in Egypt. There, during a battle, a witch saved his life, but cursed this family in doing so. She became de Cliffe's consort and bound them to the underworld.

I hope you will keep an open mind. From what I can gather, not once over the centuries have any of these dense Wycliff men asked themselves why the witch saved de Cliffe's life, why she came to England, and why de Cliffe had this marvellous tower built for her. I have never believed my husband's ranting about the tower and this family being cursed. He created his own bad luck when he turned his back on us and decided to fritter away the little we have. Men filter things through their experiences, casting everything in tones of war and aggression. Women see connections and harmony. Our families always come first.

HANNAH PAUSED and considered those words. Family, to her, had a wider connotation and included friends and those for whom she felt a responsibility. She followed the example set by her parents, and especially her mother. Lady Seraphina Miles fiercely defended those she considered family like an angry tiger with magic in her tail.

"I say, Barnes, I rather like Wycliff's mother. She cuts to the heart of things, does she not?"

The hand signalled a thumbs up like an

exhausted miner, coated in a thick layer of soot. He would need a hot bath and a scrub when they returned to the kitchen. They might need to resort to her mother's magic to clean under his short nails.

Returning to the letter, Hannah continued to read.

I SEE *the tower as a blessing. Place your hands against the stones and feel her warmth. The witch chose de Cliffe and this family. The changing scene on the tiles and the alteration of the statue in the conservatory are her attempts to make us aware of her presence. Just as the tower stands guard over the estate, she protects and watches over this family with a maternal eye. We have only to open our hearts to her message.*

"WE ARE OF ONE MIND," Hannah whispered to the previous Lady Wycliff. "What a lovely way to frame things, that this tower is a blessing. I, too, believe Kemsit has kept watch over de Cliffe's descendants, even as they scorned her and cast her as some villain in their tale. No, that is not right. The men have scorned her, but not the women."

She tapped the letter against her hand and stared at the fireplace. Hannah imagined a succession of Lady Wycliffs enjoying the calm that washed over a person in the tower room. How marvellous that at last, Kemsit's watchful eye would be acknowledged and honoured.

With Christmas so close, an idea took shape in her mind. Hannah picked up the hand and held him at eye level. "I have something to ask of you, Barnes. We need to keep this discovery a secret until Christmas Eve. Can you do that for me?"

He gave an enthusiastic thumbs up. She should have known the hand would be up for anything involving a secret, a bit of subterfuge, or a surprise. Hannah gathered up the parcel and the letters.

"Come along, then. We have much to do and Mrs Rossett will insist on giving you a good scrubbing."

The hand rose up on his stump and clutched two fingers to his palm, somewhat like a woman placing a hand over her heart.

"You like Mrs Rossett, don't you?" Hannah asked as they approached the stairs.

A finger waved up and down in a yes.

"I suspect she is rather fond of you, too. You are ever so helpful and despite the warning she issued on your first meeting, I have not yet seen her skewer you to the table with a knife."

While there could never be any sort of romantic relationship between the housekeeper and the hand—*Could there? Surely not*—Hannah did not doubt there was deep companionship. She had spied Mrs Rossett knitting an array of left-hand mittens. Work she hurriedly hid in a basket when Barnes scurried into the room. Hannah suspected there would be more than one surprise when they exchanged gifts at Christmas.

Downstairs, the study of Lady Wycliff remained mostly empty apart from some furniture draped in dust cloths. While Hannah didn't have any immediate plans to use the room since she much preferred the library, it made an excellent hiding spot. She lifted the sheet to open a drawer in the desk and slid the parcel to the very back.

"Done," she whispered. She would return later to prepare for her surprise. But first, she must take Barnes to the kitchen for a bath.

A cry went up from Mrs Rossett on seeing the state of the hand. "He looks like a coal miner! I hope you haven't made sooty footprints all over my clean floor."

The hand turned around to see where he had been. Then his knuckles drooped.

"Let's be having you over here, then." The housekeeper picked up the kettle and poured hot water into the sink.

"I am sorry, Mrs Rossett. Barnes was exploring the chimneys, in case anything had been hidden up in the brickwork," Hannah said.

The older woman shook her head. "Next time I shall give you a coal scuttle to carry him back in."

Hannah picked up the hand in her equally dirty palms and placed him on the bench. "I promise that in future, I shall use a bucket when Barnes is particular filthy. Fortunately, most of the soot brushed off on the stone of the spiral stairs and I did ensure he didn't pass too closely to any furnishings."

Leaving the hand to be thoroughly cleaned, Hannah washed her own hands and retreated to the conservatory to check on arrangements for the wedding. Pink orchids in silver pots were placed along the edges of the path where Mary would walk. Seraphina had her hands on either side of a tightly shut bloom as she whispered to the plant.

"How go the preparations?" Hannah asked.

Her mother flashed her a brief smile. "Bright pink is such an argumentative colour. This would have been far easier if Mary preferred white. But I am making headway and as long as the temperature remains constant, they have all promised to bloom tomorrow afternoon."

Hannah pondered the fickleness of orchids. If the only thing that went wrong tomorrow was an uncooperative flower, she would thank Kemsit for it.

THE DAY before Christmas dawned with clear, pale blue skies and a freezing temperature. Mary and Frank would marry in the afternoon, giving the family time to finish their preparations. Mary woke late and took breakfast on a tray in bed while Mrs Rossett and the maids prepared a bath for her. The footmen were responsible for ensuring Frank was groomed to perfection, and Barnes had volunteered to supervise. Hannah would join the women when they helped Mary dress and finalise her appearance.

Later that morning, once she ensured everything was proceeding on time, Hannah left the staff boiling water and sought out her mother. The mage and her father were settled with books in the drawing room.

"You and Sera have done a fine job in here,

Hannah. We've not had such a Christmas since you were a child." Sir Hugh raised his coffee cup to her from his spot by the fire. Sheba lay at his feet, stretched out in the warmth.

The air held a faint whiff of cinnamon that increased Hannah's merry mood when she surveyed the tree with its sparkling lights. "I merely had the idea. Mother provided the magic."

"I am only a mage," Seraphina said, putting aside her book. "This house is definitely responding to the unique magic only you possess, Hannah. There is something about you and Wycliff combined that resonates through every stone in Mireworth."

Hannah blushed at her mother's words. She loved her husband, and it gladdened her heart that her happiness infused the house. In addition, their bond with the afterlife enabled them to appreciate Kemsit and finally discover the truth about her and the tower.

"Could I prise you away from the fire, Mother? I'd like to talk to you about Kemsit." As Hannah spoke, the spaniel raised one ear, but on not hearing her name, flopped it back over again.

"Of course. Let us go visit her before I have to put the last touches to the conservatory for the wedding." Her mother rose and kissed her father's cheek on her way past.

As they walked from the drawing room and

over the tiled landscape of Duat, Hannah shared her idea. "Out in the grounds, Kemsit showed me the echo of a moment from long ago. While I only saw a few seconds of that snowball fight, both her laughter and expression spoke of her happiness and love for de Cliffe. I believe she watches over this family and that changing these tiles was her way of reaching out when the tower was concealed. I was wondering—what if I asked her for another echo, to show us what truly happened here?"

They passed under the stairs and headed to the room that opened to the drive on one side and the ground floor of the tower on the other. "It is possible," Seraphina mused, "and you seem to have a connection to her. What moment do you think would assist us?"

Once they entered the tomb, Hannah walked over to the sarcophagus and placed a hand on the lid. "I want to ask her about their last moments here. What happened when she was interred, or what prompted it?"

The only problem was that Hannah didn't know how to ask for a specific memory. Out in the garden she had been guided by instinct, wondering if her other form would be more in touch with any residue from the shadow mage.

"We can only try. While Kemsit has moved on to the Aaru, I suspect she still keeps an eye on the living realm. A request from both of us might be heard." Seraphina sat on the ground and leaned against the cool stone. Her physical form went limp, as though she had fallen asleep.

Hannah stroked the base of her throat and touched the ankh hidden under her skin. Her afterlife form enclosed her and the golden bracelets on her arms gleamed in the soft light. Her mother's soul rose from its immobile physical form and stood next to Hannah. Mother and daughter joined hands and bowed their heads.

"Show us, Kemsit, please, what happened here in your last moments," Seraphina murmured.

Seconds passed, and their only response was silence. Not even a breath stirred the tomb, as both women were in spirit form. Then, footsteps raced along the stones. A draft brushed against Hannah. Movement flashed past her eyes, too quick for her to identify. Then an echo of Kemsit shimmered beside the stone tomb and took shape. At her side, de Cliffe.

"Are you sure?" de Cliffe asked, taking Kemsit's hands in his.

Her black hair tumbled loose down her back. Her dark skin glistened in the light of a flickering torch. She wore a simple woollen robe of blood red. Hannah saw echoes of Wycliff in de Cliffe, from the tall build to the sharp angles of his face and dark eyes.

"Yes. This is the only way, my love. Your mage

council will not let us be together in this realm, and they will soon be at our gates. I shall wait for you in the Duat." She leaned forward and kissed his lips.

Sweat slicked de Cliffe's face and he had a gaunt appearance, most unlike Hannah's last glimpse of him in the garden.

Kemsit climbed into the sarcophagus and arranged her skirts. De Cliffe pressed a single rose into her hands, then he leaned in to kiss her again. "I am sorry they did not allow us to live the life we should have had. But I am grateful I had sufficient time to see my son grow into a man."

Kemsit stroked his cheek. "I will remove myself from the mages' view, but they cannot stop my influence. I will always watch over your family as though they were my own."

He turned his face to kiss her palm. "I do not know if I can bear to entomb you in here."

Kemsit lay down in the sarcophagus and rested her hands over her chest, the rose in her grasp. "Do not fear for me. This body is already dead. Have the stonemason close up the tower. Then I will activate the binding spell so they cannot disturb my remains. While you will not see me, I will always be at your side, until you are ready to pass and join me."

A grimace flashed across his features. "You will not have to wait long, my love. I feel the tumour inside me pressing on my lungs and every day I grow weaker."

The spirit echoes shimmered, the lid of the tomb slid closed, then the couple vanished from sight. A sliding and grating noise came from phantom stones that filled the doorway and blocked out the light. Chanting arose from the tomb, a flash of purple blasted upward, and the mortar and stones snapped together tight.

Silence fell and the firefly lights strung by Seraphina reappeared and sparkled around the ceiling.

"He was *dying*," Hannah said, releasing her afterlife form. Even in their enlightened times, an aftermage with a medical gift such as Timmy's would struggle to remove a tumour. There would have been little anyone could have done for de Cliffe in the twelfth century, except perhaps offer him opium to relieve his pain.

Seraphina returned to her body and stood, brushing dust from her gown. "They chose to be together in the Duat and to evade the mage council. I can well imagine the mob storming the castle with lit torches, demanding she be dragged out and burned." Seraphina curled her hands into fists, and then she released a spray of sparks into the air. The sparks took flight and wove patterns around Kemsit's tomb.

Tears moistened Hannah's eyes, and she

turned to her mother. "You will do the same when Papa's time comes."

Her mother nodded. "I cannot exist in this realm without him. But do not go worrying yourself, for you will not lose us. When that day arrives, we will await you and Wycliff in the Duat. Besides, between Timmy and me, we intend to ensure your father lives a long and healthy life."

"He will age while you will not," Hannah whispered, wondering how her mother would bear it.

Tears sparkled in her mother's gaze, turning her blue eyes to sapphires. "To me, he will always be the handsome young surgeon who was brave enough to take my wrist that first day at court, when I was doing something rather foolish."

Humour burst through Hannah. Her parents had had an odd first meeting. Her father told of how Seraphina bewitched him on sight, and that he knew in that first instance of gazing upon her that she possessed his heart and he would never love another. Thinking of all the forms that love took made ideas flare in her mind.

"One of mine for one of yours," Hannah murmured the words carved into the stone of the floor. "We took it to mean de Cliffe giving his heir to become a hound of Anubis, but what if it meant something deeper than that?"

Her mother let out a sigh. "You think Kemsit meant a de Cliffe for a shadow mage, or the child of one. You and Wycliff have found the happiness that was denied them."

"Yes." Sorrow burned Hannah's throat as she imagined what the couple had gone through. Facing a world who viewed a dead mage as a thing of evil, who could not see the beauty she could bring.

Seraphina pulled Hannah into a hug. "That we will never know for certain until we find her in the afterlife. But if Kemsit guided my hand when I asked Kitty to invite Wycliff to Lizzie's ball, then we all owe her our thanks. I doubt you two would have ever crossed paths without her intervention, and I cannot imagine a more perfect pair."

"Sometimes God, or a goddess, or a shadow mage, truly does work in mysterious ways." Hannah stared up at the ceiling and considered what to do next. "I'll not disturb her remains, now that we have seen that she holds only a rose."

"Their story is here, Hannah, in her tomb. After Christmas I will finalise the spell to reveal it." Seraphina released Hannah from the hug.

Hannah thought their story should be recorded in a journal, to be treasured and handed down in the family from this day forward. "We need to strip the outer layer from the tower so that it is revealed once more. Then Wycliff and I can begin a new history of this family, one that celebrates what de Cliffe and Kemsit achieved."

Seraphina tugged on Hannah's hand. "Let that wait until the new year. Today, we have a wedding to celebrate."

The two women headed for the conservatory and the last-minute preparations. The kitchen buzzed with activity as Mrs Rossett cooked the wedding feast. Delicious aromas made Hannah's stomach rumble, then it flip-flopped in an odd fashion. After Frank and Mary were married in the conservatory, they would celebrate with the wedding breakfast in the servants' hall—because Hannah still refused to venture into Mireworth's formal dining room.

Hannah pushed open the conservatory doors and drew in a sharp breath. Her mother had crafted a beautiful setting. The bashful orchids had opened as requested, and blooms in a bright cerise were offset by their plain white kin. Ferns dangled from hanging baskets and added sprays of rich green. Even the fish in the pond wore new colours for the day, pink and white flashing through the water. Chairs covered in simple white linen were set out in rows between the raised beds. The flower garlands the women had made were woven between them all. Her mother added a subtle wash of magic to make the blooms sparkle, and tiny lights twinkled among the lush ferns.

"Mary will love it." The faint sweet aroma of

jasmine filled the air from the climber scrambling over one wall of the conservatory.

Seraphina stood beside Hannah and hugged her. "I am sorry you did not have the magical wedding you deserved."

"I do not mind so much, as marriage has brought its own magic into my life." She would never regret marrying Wycliff, even though at the time it seemed more like a funeral. "But if you are so inclined, perhaps next year we could throw a ball here at Mireworth and invite the entire village to celebrate Christmas. We haven't touched the ballroom yet, and you can turn it into a magical landscape for me."

Seraphina winked and rubbed her hands together. "We are agreed, my child. You shall have a ball in a winter wonderland with a very special dance for you and Wycliff."

They fussed with a few minor details. Hannah straightened a chair. Seraphina had stern words for the uncooperative orchid and tweaked the hanging display of a moss. Then Hannah ensured everything was in place for the reverend.

Seraphina surveyed their work. "All we need are the bride and groom and the guests."

Everything looked perfect. Only the family and staff would attend the wedding of the shy couple.

"Let us hope the weather holds." Hannah peered up through the sparkling clean panes of the conservatory. The sky had the eerie pale hue that often preceded snow.

"I shall ensure Frank is ready if you want to check on Mary," Seraphina said.

The two women parted company. Frank dressed in the butler's room, with the assistance of Hannah's father and the footman, Victor. Hannah walked down to Mrs Rossett's comfortable room and played maid to Mary. She fussed around Mary and tweaked each curl, though Mary had insisted on arranging her own hair. She wore the pink dress that Hannah had purchased on their first trip to Mireworth.

"I shall leave you to finish here and make sure everyone is seated." Mrs Rossett kissed Mary's cheek and hustled the other maid, Hollie, from the room.

Hannah stood back to survey their work. "You are lovely, Mary."

The maid blushed and stared at the tips of her toes. With her blonde hair and fair colouring, normally somewhat ashen from fright, today she radiated happiness.

"Mother coaxed these to bloom for you." Hannah picked up a bunch of roses, their blooms the colour of clotted cream and the stems tied with a length of pink silk ribbon.

Mary took the flowers and wound one finger in the ribbon. Deep breaths made her chest heave.

The maid's gaze darted around the room as though she sought an escape route.

"Is everything all right?" Hannah asked.

Mary pulled herself up and nodded. "Yes. Just a little nervous. It's a big step, isn't it? Marrying the one who makes your heart beat faster."

Hannah smiled and took Mary's free hand. "Yes, it is a big step. And it is nerve-wracking, and exciting, and so very much worth it. You and Frank will be very happy together." Hannah would make sure of that. The odd couple deserved to find happiness in their life together.

Mary grinned. "Right. Let's get a move on, then, and get this done. I'm ever so hungry and the smells coming out of the kitchen are making my stomach rumble."

Hannah held the door open for Mary. Wycliff waited in the hall, and nodded to the maid.

"You look beautiful, Mary. Frank is a very lucky man." He held out his arm.

In a particularly bold move for the nervous maid, she had asked Wycliff if he would give her away. He had been only too happy to comply, even after Hannah whispered that Frank and Mary would be staying on.

Hannah kissed Mary's cheek and rushed ahead to take her place. Seraphina's magic turned the conservatory into a fairy-like garden. The hanging ferns glistened like emeralds. The orchids were luminescent. The water from the fountain tinkled with a soft tune as though it hid a ghost playing a pianoforte. The servants and Hannah's parents took their seats on the chairs between the garden beds.

The new vicar (older, married, and most decidedly not a selkie) waited by the terrace doors with the Bible in his hands. Frank, clad in a dark grey coat and trousers, swayed from foot to foot beside the religious man. To his credit, the vicar had only blinked twice on seeing the groom and then muttered about God crafting the perfect mate for every one of his creatures. Hannah had held her tongue. God had had no hand in crafting that particular creature.

Barnes sat on Frank's shoulder wearing the snowy white cravat that Mrs Rossett had made for him. The hand had been most insistent that he could perform the duties of best man.

Mary and Wycliff entered, and everyone uttered a sigh. The young woman glowed, her cheeks rosy and her eyes sparkling. Music arose from the pond, a beautiful and haunting tune as the bride made her way around the paths to her waiting groom.

Frank went a paler shade of yellow as he stared at Mary. Even Barnes went still on his shoulder. When they reached the altar, Wycliff placed Mary's hand in Frank's and then kissed her cheek. The stitched-together man huffed.

Wycliff seated himself beside Hannah and took her hand. The reverend performed a simple service and reading. After they sang a hymn and Hannah's father read a selection about all creatures being worthy of love, the moment came for the ring. Barnes flourished the golden band he had been clinging to. Then, with his duty done, Frank set him down on the ground and the hand scurried to sit beside Mrs Rossett.

Frank slipped the ring onto Mary's finger, and the reverend declared them to be husband and wife. Hannah wiped a tear from her eye as the monster placed a gentle kiss on the maid's lips. Beside Hannah, Barnes had his fingers laced with Mrs Rossett's. Their family found happiness in the oddest of places.

Everyone rose to offer their congratulations to the couple, and Hannah couldn't decide who blushed the most from all the kisses and hugs—Mary or Frank. Then, they adjourned to the servants' hall. The space had a festive air, decorated with garlands of fresh greenery, holly, and little silver bells.

Laughter rang out as everyone chatted. Wycliff sat at the head of the table and made the toast to the happy couple. Mrs Rossett sat in her place at the other end of the long table, while Hannah was happy to sit at her husband's right hand. After a marvellous feast and many toasts to the newlyweds, Mireworth quietened down. The footman left to drive the reverend back to his cottage. They threw rose petals over the newlyweds and Frank picked Mary up in his arms to carry her out to his room in the stables, the garden cottage not yet being ready for them.

Hannah tried to help Mrs Rossett and the staff clear away, but was shooed out. "You go through to the drawing room, milady. I'll have Hollie bring a pot of hot chocolate once we're sorted here."

Before she could marshal an argument, Wycliff took her hand and winked at the housekeeper. "I shall whisk her away, Mrs Rossett, before she decides to wash up."

"I don't mind helping." Hannah glanced at her mother, expecting to find support.

"In this, Hannah, I shall defer to Mrs Rossett." Seraphina linked arms with Sir Hugh and left the hall.

Hannah sighed. It was hard for the lady of the house to not insist on doing the dishes. Nor did it feel right to leave the staff with so much to clean up when they should all be celebrating and putting their feet up. "Very well, since I am outnumbered."

In the drawing room, Wycliff and her father settled into armchairs by the enormous tree. Presents in brightly wrapped boxes with large bows sat underneath. Hannah stared out the window as snow began to fall, covering the ground in a white blanket. The rising moon caressed the scene with a silvery touch.

"Exactly on time," her mother murmured by her side.

Hannah turned. "This is your doing?"

"Mother Nature is extremely accommodating if you ask her nicely for such things. Besides, I rather thought your first Christmas at Mireworth needed a magical touch." Seraphina leaned forward and kissed Hannah's forehead. "Merry Christmas, my dear. Why don't you give Wycliff his gift? He is eyeing that box like a small boy who suspects it contains a new set of tin soldiers."

Hannah stifled a laugh. Wycliff had spotted his name on the tag and kept glancing at it from the corner of his eye. The family always exchanged one gift on Christmas Eve, and she would continue that tradition at Mireworth.

Hannah picked up the blue-and-black-striped box from under the tree and carried it to Wycliff. "Merry Christmas," she said as she handed it over.

His brow furrowed. "You did not have to buy me a gift."

"I didn't." Which only made his frown deepen.

He pulled the ribbon and undid the bow. Then he lifted the lid and stared within. "I don't understand." He pulled out a smaller, teal-coloured box that read *To Hannah* on the note attached.

"You will understand shortly." She had to bite her lip to keep from laughing. It had taken an inordinate amount of self-control merely to wait until this moment to give him the box.

"Merry Christmas," he said, pressing the smaller gift into her hands.

She sat before him on the footstool and glanced at him from under lowered lashes. Then she undid the ribbon and slid the top to one side. The contents were concealed by pink tissue paper. Hannah picked up an end and pulled it away. Firelight caught an object and rainbows spun around the room.

"Impossible!" Wycliff exclaimed.

Hannah picked up the necklace, needing two hands due to its weight. "Would you?"

She turned her body away from Wycliff. He took the heavy necklace from her hands and placed it around her neck, then tied the black velvet ribbons at her nape. "How did you conjure the Wycliff family necklace? For it cannot be the real one."

She turned back to face him and placed one hand on the central pink diamond shaped like the middle of a flower. Diamond petals surrounded it, and the heavy bloom rested over the golden ankh hiding under her skin. Smaller diamonds had been expertly crafted into twisted vines of leaves that held the central flower, and the diamond foliage rested across her collarbone. "It is as real as you and I. Your mother hid it in the tower. Barnes and I found it concealed in the chimney, along with a note for you."

Hannah moved aside the tissue paper and revealed the folded sheet of paper with its seal still intact. On the front a single name...*Jonas*.

His hand shook as he took the page and slid his thumb under the seal. He scanned the contents and then raised his gaze to Hannah. He swallowed a lump in his throat before reading out loud.

. . .

*J*ONAS, *my darling, your father's demons will consume anything of value in this house, but he shall not have this. These diamonds do not belong to him, nor to any Lord Wycliff. They are a legacy to be handed through the generations to each Lady Wycliff, a gift to us from a long ago de Cliffe's lover. The gems were brought to this country by the witch, and she turned them into this necklace. I hope that one day, you will place these around your wife's neck and she will know Kemsit's touch. She has watched over this family through the centuries.*

Your loving mother,

Frances

SERAPHINA SNORTED. "La! The women of this family knew that Kemsit was their guardian. At least Wycliff here had the sense to form his own opinion and listened to our Hannah."

Hannah stroked her hand over the diamonds as a thought occurred to her. "Do you think these are from the Duat, like the others we have recovered?" Did she wear a collar of *soul shards*, as she called the precious gems that remained after she freed a trapped sliver of soul?

Wycliff shook his head. "I suspect we will never know. But it is possible that Anubis gave them to her. The gods do seem to pay their servants in gems."

Hollie entered carrying a tray, and set it down on a low table. Hannah knelt on the rug between it and the fire to pour the hot chocolate.

A glow emanated from the wooden box on the writing desk. Seraphina excused herself to open the lid. The ensorcelled box allowed her to correspond with other mages and the glow meant a new missive had appeared inside it. She read the sheet of paper and glanced at Hannah. Dropping it back to the desk, she walked to the window. With her eyes closed, her mother turned her face to the silvery caress of the moon.

Hannah left Wycliff to approach the silent mage. "Mother? Is everything all right?"

A sigh heaved through her mother, and she turned with eyes glistening with tears. "Lord Pendlebury has passed. I rather liked him. He was always a voice of reason on the mage council."

"Oh, I am sorry to hear that." As Hannah recollected, Pendlebury had been the speaker of the council, and that role would now fall to another.

Seraphina wiped a tear from the corner of her eye. "There is more. His powers have been reborn in Kent, not far from where Lizzie and Harden are." Before Hannah could draw a breath to comment, her mother went on, "In a girl."

Hannah's hand went to her mouth as she imagined a villain creeping through the night to smother the child and deprive her of the opportunity to make her mark on the world. "I am sure Harden will do all he can to protect her."

Seraphina nodded. "Let us hope his protection is not needed. The council has passed a motion condemning such barbaric practices and all mage-gifted children, whatever their gender, are to be allowed the chance to flourish."

Relief surged through Hannah. "That is wonderful news and will herald a new era."

"There is more. They have requested that I become her mentor when she reaches the age of five. I will refuse, of course." Her mother turned back to the white wonderland outside the window. With a swipe of her hand, snow swirled into a ball and made the base of a snowman.

"Why would you refuse? What an opportunity to ensure the child learns all she needs to know to face this cruel world. How could you entrust her training to another..." Hannah's voice trailed off as she met her mother's gaze. Only now did it occur to Hannah that her mother had never mentored another mage. She had always assumed the council didn't want a woman training a man. But what if her mother had refused previous offers? "Oh, Mother. You didn't want to bring a gifted child into our household."

"You are my daughter, and I love you most

fiercely. Never would I want you to feel replaced if I mentored a child mage." Seraphina reached out for Hannah and took her hands.

"Once, I admit I harboured a small amount of jealousy that I am devoid of magic," Hannah confessed. "But I have found my own. I can travel between this realm and the next. I bring peace to lost souls, helping them on their journey to the afterlife."

Her mother had been wrenched from her family home at a tender age and given to a mage who treated her no better than a servant. Hannah thought it somewhat barbaric that the young mages were expected to begin training at five, but could see the benefit of ensuring they had some control over their growing power. At least they could offer the gifted girl a safe haven in which to thrive.

Seraphina hugged her daughter. "Thank you. If it will not cause you pain, I would be honoured to mentor this child. Perhaps she could spend some time here? Mireworth and Kemsit's tower seem a fitting place to raise a new mage and teach her our ways."

Hannah beamed. "I would be privileged to welcome her into our home. She would not be alone here and will find at least one other to play with." Hannah passed a hand over her stomach.

Seraphina gasped and glanced over her

shoulder to see if the men were looking. Then she leaned closer to Hannah. "Are you...?"

"I suspect so, but I am not entirely sure yet. Wycliff does not know. I want to be certain first." A quiver of worry wormed through her. "And it is a fraught and dangerous path I take, with no certainty upon it."

"With me, Kemsit, and Anput watching over you, I have every certainty that you will both be fine should Mother Nature choose to bless you," Seraphina murmured. Then mischief sparkled in her eyes. "What exciting times lie ahead."

For some reason, the ghost of Lisbeth passed through Hannah's mind, as she saw a young boy and girl laughing as they ran along the hallways of this old house. Sometimes, if love wasn't allowed to flourish in one time, it sprouted up in another and found the circumstances it needed to thrive. "I believe Mireworth will finally be the home she was always meant to be."

Seraphina brushed her hands over the glass of the window and added a body and head to the snowman. Then twigs drifted from the nearby trees to form arms and a nose.

"If mages could alter time, would you?" Hannah asked.

Her mother's eyes glinted in the low light. "Yes. I would protect every single girl mage and ensure she reached adulthood. Certain prejudices have festered for too long unchallenged. While we have finally created a new world for others like me, we will never know how differently things might have evolved."

"Imagine if all women mages were able to bear gifted offspring like the Crows," Hannah murmured.

She thought of how not long after Kemsit had come to England, a girl mage was raised in the woods by an old man who protected and hid the child. The shifter hunter sent to end her life instead fell in love, and became her fiercest protector. She gave him three daughters, each child blessed with magic and able to shift form into a crow. No mage since had ever produced magical offspring; their power always skipped a generation.

"Mother Nature keeps some secrets to herself, and we do not know if that mage crafted a spell to gift her children with magic, or if it was a reward for all that she had endured. But whatever happens going forward, this child will have a choice." Seraphina hugged Hannah and placed a kiss on the top of her head.

Hannah returned to her husband and leaned against his side. In another week, when she was certain, she would tell him her news. Perhaps on New Year's Eve, when they shared their hopes for the coming year.

"Happy?" Wycliff murmured as he raised her hand to kiss her knuckles.

"Yes." Love filled her. For her husband, her parents, and the unconventional family they created at the old estate. Whatever delights or challenges the future brought, they would face them together.

History. Magic. Family.

I do hope you enjoyed Hannah's last adventure. If you would like to dive deeper into the world, or learn more about the odd assortment of characters that populate it, you can join the community by signing up at:

https://tillywallace.com/newsletter/

ABOUT THE AUTHOR

Tilly writes whimsical historical fantasy books, set in a bygone time where magic is real. Her books combine vintage magic and gentle humour with an oddball cast. Through fierce friendships her characters discover that in an uncertain world, the most loyal family is the one you create.

To be the first to hear about new releases and special offers, sign up at:
https://tillywallace.com/newsletter/

Tilly would love to hear from you:
https://tillywallace.com
tilly@tillywallace.com

facebook.com/tillywallaceauthor

bookbub.com/authors/tilly-wallace

ALSO BY TILLY WALLACE

For the most complete and up to date list of books,
please visit the website

Available series:

Tournament of Shadows

Manner and Monsters

Highland Wolves

9 780047 360433 2